Costanza is unsure of what to think about this new man at her door.

"Perhaps your overseer would be so kind as to give me a tour of the premises. Later, Costanza, you might enjoy looking over some of my merchandise. I have wonderful, finely tooled leather goods and every sort of savory cheese imaginable."

Costanza, shocked by the man's boldness and reference to business, found herself at a loss for words. Here was a complete stranger asking to look around the estate. He could have an ulterior motive. Even a dashing barone could be a spy. And, of course, a merchant would want to take advantage of this unique opportunity—to sell goods to a poor widow in a weakened frame of mind. *Ah,* she recalled, *we still have the money I would have paid for the ransom. Again we have been snatched from the jaws of poverty.*

"Forgive me, Costanza. I did not mean to intrude. I am always interested in the layout and structuring of an estate. From the expression on your face, I discern a reluctance. . ."

"Yes, Signore," admitted Costanza. "I keep a close guard on the property. With reason. Please understand."

Antonio finished the contents of his porcelain cup, set it on the saucer, and leaned toward Costanza. "I understand fully, Costanza. You are a very strong woman to know when to refuse a request. I admire that."

"One does what one must," said Costanza, somewhat coolly. *Who is this man who calls me Costanza so easily—is outrageously bold, yet gracious?*

BARBARA YOUREE has authored four children's books as well as numerous stories and articles. This is her second **Heartsong Presents** novel. She is a contributing editor of *Potpourri, A Magazine of the Literary Arts*, and a docent at the Nelson-Atkins Museum of Art. She makes her home in Kansas.

HEARTSONG PRESENTS

Books by Barbara Youree
HP416—Both Sides of the Easel

with you. Follow his directions. Go! Be off!"

The young man, who had already saddled a horse, snatched the remaining ax from its hook and headed toward the choice vineyards. The selected crew followed without further questions.

The rest stood embarrassed, awaiting orders from this woman who now commanded with as much authority as her husband, the marchese, had in past years.

"Take the wagons and carriages to the Nera River and fill the vats. Then rush them to the men fighting the blaze. You will need to make many trips until the fire is finally extinguished."

The odor of smoke hung ominously in the wintry darkness.

"Here comes Sandro. He will direct the vehicles."

Sandro dropped an armload of grain sacks into an empty wine vat and leapt with unaccustomed agility onto the lead wagon, eager to fulfill his new responsibility.

The woman watched her commands turn into action. Suddenly everyone was gone, and all sound came from a far distance. In this brief pause, Costanza surveyed the vast area of eighty hectares or more, rocky hills and fertile valleys—the largest of the three seigniories around Terni. For the first time she realized how widespread the fires were. The dry winter certainly exposed the land to fire from a variety of causes: a campfire not totally extinguished, a lantern left unattended. Travelers often passed through the estate on the narrow road that cut through the hills. Strange that the fires sprang from multiple origins.

Costanza stood, hands on hips, her short form planted firmly in her roomy boots, wisps of hair curling about her temples, and the red ribbon fluttering in the frosty breeze. She watched, as against the threatening glow silhouettes of wagons rumbled far off to the north, and young Albret dashed with his followers to the east.

"Please, God, keep them safe," she pleaded while smoke stung her eyes and burned her nostrils.

two

Morning broke through a solemn haze as two men and Anabella dipped their buckets in the chilling Nera and filled the last vat on the wagon before it headed toward the vineyards.

"Now, my pretty one, get back to the kitchen where you belong," jeered Anslo, the older man and wagon driver. He rubbed the back of his rough hand across her flushed cheek and winked. "What a prize some gent will have in you. Ripe as a peach you are for plucking."

Anabella pulled back repulsed. Anslo stepped up on the wagon beside the other workman and turned toward her with a grin. Then they rumbled off. She wiped her cheek with her sleeve and walked quickly along the riverbank. *How stupid of me to come here,* she thought. *I saw myself only as another pair of hands needed to work.* Indeed, it was a breach of custom for a girl to be alone in the company of a group of men, many of whom she hardly knew.

The house servants had burned the grasses around the castle in only a few hours while the women provided them with buckets of water for control. Anabella, feeling invigorated by their success, had hopped a ride on a wagon headed for the river, where she worked as hard as any of the men through the night. Mostly she filled the vats alongside Sandro. Her whole life he had been like a grandfather to her and—since the death of Lorenzino—a protective father besides. His presence had given her a false sense of security. Where was Sandro now? She hadn't seen him for nearly an hour.

Though exhausted, faint from hunger, and trembling from Anslo's advances, she frantically searched the bank for her beloved friend. He would not have gone to the vineyards on any of the wagon trips as he was charged with supervising from this end. Her arms and shoulders ached from the night's work. Her dress was torn from briers, her hands scratched and streaked with mud. She pulled her hood over damp, stringy hair and sank to her knees. Dry weeds snapped beneath her ample skirts. "Father God," she murmured, "may Sandro not be harmed." She looked to the east and saw the dying glow of the remnant fire. Above it, through the smoke, rose the glow of a new day's sun. "And thank You, Lord, for saving our home and perhaps some of the vineyards."

She rose and retraced her steps, searching earnestly. Suddenly she came across Sandro's body, lying prone in the dry undergrowth, his bucket still in his grasp.

"Oh, Sandro! No!" she wailed, rushing to his side. She knelt beside the old man and sought frantically for signs of life.

&

Still the inferno raged, closing in on the vineyards. The men chopped and swore. Several times as they defensively set fire to the dry vines, the blaze would strike out in an errant direction by an unexpected shift of the wind. They then beat the flames with the soggy grain sacks as Costanza had instructed.

Just at a point when they had run out of water, a brush fire whipped around two men, cutting off all means of escape.

"Help! We're trapped. Help us!" screamed a family man named Massetti.

Albret, being swift of thought as well as deed, urged his horse to leap the smaller flames. "Hold out!" he cried.

Alas! The horse panicked and fled in the opposite direction. Albret jumped off.

"Beat the low flames with the flat side of your axes!" He joined in, carrying out his own order. When an escape path finally opened, he and a few others rushed in and carried the two to safety, laying them gently on the grass until hands could be freed to tend them. One was badly burned after his cloak had caught fire; the other, singed and spent. Both suffered from the searing smoke they had breathed into their lungs.

At that moment, Anslo and his partner arrived with the new supply of water. As throughout the whole ordeal, the horses were spooked as they approached the fire and had to be loosed from their burden and tied. Precious time was lost as the men called forth the last bit of strength from their already strained muscles. They pushed the heavy wagon down a slight incline toward the fire. Water splashed over them, feeling delicious at first, but then chilling in the night air. When finally at close range, each plunged a sack into a vat and ran toward the flames, beating them back with renewed spirits. The larger conflagration continued to roar toward them. They repeated their fight, sloshing the sacks again and again in a mechanical rhythm. At last the small backfire began to die down, leaving only smoldering whiffs of smoke.

With energy now totally sapped, the laborers stood in silence, helplessly watching the approach of the larger fire. Would all their efforts, hours of backbreaking work, pay off? Would Costanza's plan work? Would the sacrifice of the choice vines hold and deprive the monster of fuel? Or would the fire only pause, gather strength, and devour them?

They watched.

Finally someone whispered, "It's slowing."

"It's hit our scorched earth," said another, moments later.

They waited.

"Thanks be to God," breathed Albret.

The blaze began to abate, but all knew it would be hours before they could sleep. Flare-ups would need to be squelched.

Albret checked on his two patients. The one with severe burns lay in shock. The other was groaning in pain.

"Take these men on a wagon back to the castle. Signora Costanza will know what to do," said Albret.

The men began making pallets with their cloaks on the bed of the wagon.

"Signora Costanza?" said one, sneering. "How could a

marchesa know anything beyond embroidery?"

"She gave us orders like a ship's captain," responded another.

"Our marchesa has treated the sick and wounded before," Albret said. "That year she stayed in Rome after Lorenzino died—she worked tirelessly there in hospitals. She knows a good deal about caring for people."

The men lifted their anguished comrades onto the pallets. A few others with minor burns and scrapes were encouraged to climb aboard.

"Sandro must still be at the river," Albret mused aloud. "He's not able to walk back to the castle. I'll go for him, take him home, and bring all of you food and drink. We will take turns getting some rest. It will require several days to keep things under control and assess the damage." He took the smoke-blackened wedding carriage and headed toward the river.

The youth had performed his assigned duties well. He appeared every inch a commander of men, tall and straight. His dark brown hair hung just below his ears, and his clean-shaven face and the set of his jaw portrayed intelligence and decisiveness. But not everyone admired his leadership.

"Arrogant upstart," growled Anslo. "Don't know why that woman put a child in charge here."

The others turned away, too tired to argue, though most had found a new respect for both Signora Costanza and her selected commander over them.

&

Nearly a full day passed. Costanza leaned back on a stack of down pillows, exhausted. The wall tapestry hung motionless once again, the hunters on their white steeds frozen in their historic tableau. Anabella sat on the edge of the bed and held her mother's hand. Her long, dark hair now fell in lustrous ringlets over her shoulders. Both had bathed and wore white lace-trimmed muslin gowns. The faces of both were rounded with clear-cut features, large eyes, and full lips. One bore the smooth olive skin of youth. On the other, the olive skin showed the fine lines of happiness and grief that only experience could write.

"I am so sorry, Mother," the girl said. "I did not think. You should not have had to worry about me with all the other— But there were plenty of women to fill the buckets for the men. Some were complaining about the cold and indeed would have gone back to their warm beds had I not shamed them into staying."

"I was frantic with worry," said Costanza with a sigh. "They told me you had been missing for hours. Anything could have happened to you among all those men, many of whom we still do not know well. But I could not leave those who were hurt."

"I know."

"Where were you, Anabella?"

"I thought I would be more useful dipping water into the vats, so I headed toward the river and caught a ride on one of the wagons. In truth, they needed my help. Please forgive me, Mother."

"You are forgiven, my child, though you did tempt danger with your adventure. And it was you who found poor Sandro?"

"Yes, Albret arrived with the carriage soon after, and both of us lifted him in. He is so light; it was no effort. Albret drove us to the castle where we found your infirmary." Indeed, Costanza had set up a makeshift area to care for the injured, inside the north entrance at the back of the castle.

"Albret? I never saw Albret."

"He dashed off as soon as he lay Sandro on the straw mat. You were so busy, spooning warm soup into your patients. Mother, do you think Sandro will live through the night? I do not know how long he had been lying facedown by the river. I love him so."

"I know." Costanza hesitated to say more. "Pico is staying in my infirmary. He will give him the care I recommended. Most of those we treated are in their own beds tonight. All they needed was some rest and food—and some salve for minor burns. We have only three other patients left, and I believe they will all do well. One has a broken arm. Another managed to split his foot with his own ax. But only one with severe burns—his cloak caught fire."

"Mother, our little infirmary made me think of that year we were away from Terni, in Rome, after Father died."

"Yes, I thought the same, Anabella. Remember how we cared for the sick in the city hospitals?"

"And took bread to the homeless on the streets."

"And visited those in the prison Tor."

"Most of all, I remember little Elena, the orphan that Marco brought home to live with us for awhile. Until that family from the church adopted her," said Anabella.

"It was a difficult time. Marco took such good care of us. I still find it hard to believe that Jacopo would confiscate this castle and seigniory after Lorenzino cut him from his will for his evil deeds."

"I hardly knew my half brother. Do you think, Mother, that Jacopo was murdered for his money, as they said, or for some other reason?"

"That I do not know, dear daughter, but I must confide something to you." Costanza suddenly sat up straight in bed. Lines of worry creased her brow, replacing the relative calm. "At the end of the day, when all was finally under control, Albret told me there was some evidence that this terrible conflagration was more than just the result of the dry winter. We may have enemies. Our way of life may again be in jeopardy."

"How could that be? You and Father, as well as generations of Bilivertis before us, except for Jacopo, have been known for benevolence and kindness," said Anabella. "Even Albret could be wrong," she added.

The blush and faint smile that passed across the face of the girl did not go unnoticed by her mother. "We shall see" was her only comment.

"It could have been so much worse," said Anabella.

"Most of the vineyards are gone," said Costanza, shifting her pillows and falling back into them. "We will survive the winter—there should be enough food in storage for all, but the animals will not fare as well. The grasses are charred, and I do not yet know the condition of the haystacks."

"Mother, you surprise me. I've never heard you use such a calculating business tone."

"Someone must calculate. And I am the senior Biliverti, female or not. Marco should be proud of his mother, don't you agree?"

"Yes, and you were a veritable Joan of Arc today, racing about giving orders. You were amazing!"

Costanza smiled.

"You looked ready for battle in that moth-eaten old surcoat and Father's big boots." Anabella laughed, then kissed her mother's forehead. "Good night. Sleep well, Mother."

"I am truly tired. Good night, Anabella. You too played a heroine's role."

The daughter slipped out and closed the door softly.

Costanza blew out the candle at her bedside. "Joan of Arc, indeed," she scoffed aloud, untying the bedraggled red ribbon and loosing her dark, but gray-tinged, hair. She stretched her arm out across the empty place on the other side of the bed, allowed two warm tears to trickle down to the pillows, and wearily fell asleep.

three

Antonio Turati stood—legs planted like pillars, arms crossed—facing Julius, seller of textiles. Antonio's attire announced his noble position as a Florentine patrician and merchant entrepreneur—soft leather boots, black tights, embroidered white silk doublet, and a black velvet cloak, thrown jauntily over his left shoulder—indeed a striking figure, this *barone*.

He awaited samples of fabric he had requested. When a worker arrived with them, he examined the wool and rubbed it between his hands to determine its texture. The silk he assessed by gently caressing it with thumb and forefinger. As he scanned the bolts of cloth stacked to the rafters of the long warehouse, he mentally calculated the worth of the purchase.

Towering over the older man with whom he came to negotiate, he declared, "Julius, I'll take this whole lot of fine woolen cloth and twenty bolts of dyed silk." He indicated with the hilt of his dress sword his selections. "Although your silks remain of superior quality, I note, with some regret, that the woolens fall somewhat short in the softness of weave my clientele in Rome desire." Antonio stroked his short beard to a point.

"You are aware, Signore, of the drought that affected our sheep—"

"Yes, of course, my good man; but nonetheless, this is the generous amount I am prepared to offer in concluding our business." Antonio emptied two bags of gold *scudi* onto the wooden table.

Julius motioned for his clerk to come and count the coins. The two men stood silently until the clerk announced the sum.

"But you rob me, Signore," the seller exclaimed in mock disbelief, knowing full well that Antonio held an impeccable reputation for fairness and exactitude.

"I can always take my business a few paces down the Via Calimala," Antonio said with a note of finality. He reached over to gather up the money.

"No, no," Julius said as he waved his hands over the coins. "It will be enough to feed my hungry servants—even if my own little ones must go without jam."

Ignoring the lament, Antonio extended his hand to seal the deal. Both men recognized the end of the bargaining game, and each was secretly most satisfied.

Antonio changed his tone and relaxed his stance. "While our servants are loading the merchandise onto my mules and carriages, let us go to the little *ristorante* overlooking the Arno and partake of a noontime meal."

இ

The air was chilly in spite of sunshine this winter afternoon. Antonio and Julius made their way on foot down the Corso dei Tintori where raw wool hung out to dry. They passed women and girls combing, carding, spinning, and winding the fibers that supported much of the economy of Florence.

As they took a table next to an open window in the little ristorante, a faint odor of ammonia wafted up from the pens and racks where young men were washing fleece in the river Arno.

"The wool industry increases daily even as the trade in silk declines," Antonio commented, fishing for information.

"Yes, wool will always thrive even in bad years. As to silk, there is none more luxurious outside of Asia than what we produce right here in Florence. But," said Julius, leaning across the table and wagging his finger, "our antiquated silk guild controls wages and prevents us from competing fairly with France." The leather-faced older man enjoyed flaunting his knowledge. He ran his fingers through his white hair and looked around to see who might be observing them. He hoped—since this was an establishment he frequented—that many would notice he was a guest of the renowned barone.

"I see. In the spring I will make a journey to France and am thinking of going up to Lyon to purchase silk there. Our aristocrats who buy in bulk have been demanding it. But, never fear, my good man, I can still find markets for your exquisite silk fabric."

Julius smiled with satisfaction. The waiter brought steaming platefuls of boiled marrows, a Pecorino cheese, some local figs, and goblets of Florentine drink.

"Ah, nothing better than simple country fare," said Antonio as he dipped freshly baked bread in olive oil. "And these little ones you spoke of, who must go without their jam; they are grandchildren, I presume?"

"Six of them," Julius answered with pride. "Four boys, two girls, all healthy and smart as merchants. And you, my dear *barone*, will there never be little ones around your table?"

Suddenly Antonio became somber. The smiling lines around his eyes tightened, and the graying mustache that adorned his handsome face appeared to droop. "I was married once," he confided. "Lovely, lovely Margherita. The best of women. She died giving birth to—to our son."

"You have a son, Signore?"

Antonio was far away in another place and time as he stared out across the Arno, across the red tile roofs and the majestic dome of the duomo to the hills beyond. "No, I was very young and poor then. I sheared sheep and worked in the industry twelve hours a day. I left little Toni in the care of a woman who had eight children herself. She nursed him along with her own *bambini*. But he was small and weak. Then—he was no more."

"I am sorry," said Julius, embarrassed to have brought up the subject. "It is hard to imagine the prosperous *barone* ever poor. Ever having the problems of humanity. . ."

" 'Tis true." Antonio returned to the present. "I leave for Rome on the morrow. After ridding myself of most of my merchandise there, I will load my mule train with cheeses and leather goods and head back to this fair city."

The men finished their meal in silence. Antonio regretted allowing himself to share his personal grief with someone he only enjoyed sparring with over business matters. He had exposed his inner soul and left a crack in his exterior façade— a façade that showed a man with all things firmly under control and a reputation, not only of fairness and honesty, but also of brilliance in understanding the markets and skill in negotiation. A man everyone assumed to always get what he wanted.

Finally Julius wiped his mouth. "Will you pass through Terni? I understand three large seigniories employ most of the townspeople there. Should be a good market."

"Well, yes, I could stop in Terni on my return. Lorenzino Biliverti was once one of my most cherished clients. He was a jovial sort but took business transactions very seriously. His seigniory held some of the best vineyards in all the Italian states. He tended them with great care, personally overseeing the entire operation. But when he died suddenly, his son Jacopo neglected not only the vineyards but the livestock and workers as well. According to rumor, he ousted his step-mother, Lorenzino's second wife, and her children, leaving them to beg on the streets of Rome. At least, that is what I heard. I have not been to Terni in the three years since."

"I'm sure the villagers will be eager to tell you the rest of the story," Julius said with a chuckle.

"No doubt. I think the wife's name was Constantina—no, Costanza. Of course, I had no occasion to meet her. His younger son, Marco, was home, however, the last time I stopped at the castle. I remember he selected some fine woolen cloth—probably from your warehouse—to have made into gar-ments to wear in Padua at the university. A most charming young man—interested in science, I believe."

After a pause of some minutes, he rose from the table. "I am sure my men have finished loading and had time to get something to eat from the street vendors."

"I hear the villa on your country estate has been completed, Signore. Is it far from the outskirts of town?" said Julius.

"Far enough. It is on the southern side, in the direction of Rome. We will spend the night there. By the way, good man, when I return, I will invite you and your wife to come out for a few days. I have a wonderful chef, gifted in all Tuscany cuisine. I will take you on a tour of the villa—ill furnished as it presently is. Would you like that, Julius?"

"Oh, yes, Signore. My wife will be delighted." Julius beamed. He looked around again, hoping someone he knew had heard this invitation from the esteemed barone.

four

An ominous cloud settled over the Biliverti household. The fire, indeed, had destroyed virtually all the fine vineyards. The cattle refused to eat from the remaining haystacks that reeked of smoke. Little grass remained for them.

Then one night Costanza awoke suddenly to a faraway sound of cattle bawling. She lay there in rigid stillness, listening. The bellowing came not from their usual place of rest for the night but from across the Nera River. The sounds became fainter. She rushed to Pico's room and sent him to the outbuildings to round up a posse. By the time they headed out into the darkness, the bawling ceased. In the light of dawn, the men tried to find a trail of the stolen beasts, but, alas, the dry, packed earth revealed no trace. Perhaps it was a merciful theft. The bandits had gained only animals near starvation.

Worst of all the many troubles, Sandro had died in his sleep, even while Costanza watched over him in the little makeshift infirmary. The man with the most severe burns died within a day, but Sandro lingered a week, never regaining consciousness. Anabella and Pico took turns during the day caring for him as Costanza had other crises almost daily that demanded her full attention. But she alone stayed with him through the nights, napping and awakening to his groans. The two funerals so close together, both arranged by Costanza herself, drained her strength. Disputes arose among the kitchen help, and Costanza was forced to choose a head chef to replace Sandro.

Anabella, anguished at Sandro's death, felt she had twice lost a father. She insisted on wearing black lace draped over her head and face and spent hours praying in the family chapel.

Costanza now sat at Lorenzino's desk going over the ledgers. Her husband, like other men, had spared his wife the concern of financial matters. In fact, it would have appeared improper to inform a woman of such accounts. Even though this task now fell to their son, Marco, Costanza felt that, in his absence, she must gain an understanding of their assets.

Sadness mixed with warm memories of better times as she caressed the orderly pages, so clearly and neatly penned by her dear husband's hand—plantings, prunings, harvests, inventories of tools and supplies, servants' wages. A notation of every calf birthed, every sheep shorn, even the number of eggs gathered—up to the very day of his death. Then scrawled across the next page: *I, Jacopo Biliverti, am the marchese of this seigniory, master at last!!!*

No records followed for over a year. Costanza turned the pages frantically, leaving sentiment behind. Suddenly she found, in Marco's scholarly hand, a new list of servants, mixed with only a few, like Sandro, who had remained loyal even under Jacopo's usurpation. In an effort to follow his father's methods of bookkeeping, Marco had assessed the damages, listed repairs and new plantings, and made a financial accounting.

Costanza relaxed at noting her son's efficiency and leaned back in the large, leather-covered chair. She closed her eyes and reminisced over that pleasant time in spring when she and Anabella had finally returned with Marco from their year's exile in Rome. Her son, a good man like his father, brought order and security back to the seigniory. His lovely new wife, Bianca, made the large rooms ring once more with joy and laughter.

Anabella adored Bianca and begged to learn all her beauty secrets. They braided each other's hair and chatted together as sisters. The fact that Bianca was an accomplished artist in a male-dominated field fascinated the girl. Anabella would bring her needlework to Bianca's studio and sit by her at the easel, marveling at her skill as a painter.

The new marchesa had also brought with her a personal servant, Sylvia, and Sylvia's handsome and gifted son, Albret Amaseo. Costanza quickly noted how the eyes of her daughter sparkled in the young man's presence. She must remind Marco to begin the search for a suitable husband for her.

That first year back home had been a pleasant one. Marco tended to be more frugal than his father but supervised all aspects of life on the estate with the same scrupulous attention to detail. But Costanza knew how he yearned to return to his studies in Padua. In the fall he set everything in order at the castle and took leave of a few months for him and his wife to pursue their own dreams. That, of course, is how it should be. A mother is pleased to see her son find his own way.

Enough of this reverie. Costanza must study Marco's financial notations. The household money was nearly exhausted. She needed to know just how vast the Biliverti fortune was, held in the Medici Bank in Rome.

At first, she trustingly searched over the pages. Then, puzzled, she checked the figures on the previous page. Perhaps Marco had neglected to add the zeros. Gradually, the numbers began to form a startling message.

"This cannot be! We have been reduced to paupers," she said, mutely moving her lips.

Costanza closed the ledger and left the room, locking the door with the key from her belt. Trembling with anxiety, she made her way down the long hall to the little chapel. So many bad events had occurred that it seemed heavenly protection had deserted her. Nevertheless, there was no one but God to turn to.

The chapel door stood open, revealing her daughter kneeling in prayer at the altar. Shafts of blue, red, and golden light streamed through the stained glass and fell across the girl's flowing hair and smooth cheek.

Heavenly sunshine is blessing her, thought Costanza. Then

she raised her eyes and looked through the opened shutters to the charred hills beyond. *But a curse seems to be falling upon us!*

"Anabella," she called softly.

The girl arose and removed the black veil. "I am at peace, Mother. Sandro is in the arms of Jesus. I must mourn him no further."

Costanza threw her arms around her daughter and held her closely. "God is good, dear Anabella. He will see us through all our troubles." She squeezed her eyes tightly to keep back tears and tried to believe in God's mercy.

"I know that is true, Mother. But when will Marco and Bianca return? I do miss them so."

"I will pen a message to them this very day. I hate to cut his studies short again, and I'm sure Bianca is painting portraits in nearby Venice, but we do need. . ."

"Yes, Mother."

"Now it is my turn to pray," she said with a sense of urgency. She envied her daughter's simple faith—a faith that allowed her to envision Sandro in the arms of Jesus. Costanza wished she could derive the same comfort of certitude that God's love always surrounded them—this unquestioning belief of a trusting child.

"I will be in Bianca's studio, embroidering scarves for my trousseau," Anabella said almost cheerfully and embraced her mother once more before taking her leave.

In the depths of despair over the ledger findings and exhausted from her never-ending responsibilities, Costanza knelt before the altar and poured her heart out to almighty God.

☙

On the morrow, Clarice tapped lightly on the open door of Lorenzino's study. Costanza sat puzzling over the figures and notes Marco had made in the ledger, trying to discern a more favorable conclusion.

"What is it, Clarice?" she said without looking up.

"Please, Signora, a gentleman is at the gate, representing a Signore Sculli, who wishes to speak to you on an important matter he would not divulge to me."

Another crisis, thought Costanza. "Show him to the reception room. I will be with him shortly. No, that would not be seemly. Please find one of my trusted male servants and ask him to join me at the reception room door."

❧

Costanza was surprised to find Albret standing at the door. "So, Albret, you are the one to whom falls this dubious honor," she said. "I simply require a man, an observant and intelligent man like you, to stand by as a witness to whatever this matter is about. You need do nothing more. Agreed?"

"Of course, Signora. I am here, as always, to do your bidding." He opened the door, bowed slightly, and allowed the lady to precede him.

Inside stood a middle-aged man with a reddish beard, wearing ill-fitting, though expensive, clothing. He was nervously fingering a row of books on a mantle shelf. "What an impressive array of tomes you have, Marchesa. Do you—?"

"Signora will do. What are you here to discuss, Signore?" interrupted Costanza, indignant that a total stranger would take the liberty to touch objects in the room uninvited.

"As you wish, Signora Biliverti. I note you have had some misfortune of late. I see much of your land burned. What an unfortunate disaster! And the death of your dear son, Jacopo, so soon after the loss of your esteemed husband. My condolences."

"Jacopo was my stepson, and that was over a year ago. His mother died when he was a child. Now, my misfortunes aside; what brings you here? And, by the way, I am not acquainted with the name Sculli," Costanza said tersely, irritated at the man's boldness and presumption.

"I am Piero Sculli, of the honorable Sculli family from the Italian state of Tuscany, an agent for my younger brother, Niccolini. Our estate is near Siena. I am amazed that you are unaware of our long-standing reputation. I offer you, however, these three signed letters of commendation that should set your mind at ease." He bowed courteously.

"Please sit down," offered Costanza. The two sat facing each other with Albret standing behind the lady's chair.

"To get to the point, you have a daughter, Anabella by name, I believe." Albret shifted his stance. "Of marriageable age, I believe."

"She is a mere thirteen years."

"Of marriageable age. The Sculli name is a very old and honorable one, as is that of Biliverti. We propose melding these two great families into one. There will be advantages for both, I am sure. I desire, rather, Niccolini desires, to begin negotiations immediately. I presume her father has invested for her dowry. Would you have your servant call your daughter to stand before me?"

"Anabella is presently in mourning."

"For her brother Jacopo?"

"Half brother. No, she is not mourning him."

"Let us not make this a guessing game, Signora. If another member of the family has died, please let it be known."

"I need to take your proposal under consideration, Signore. I will discuss the matter with my son, Marco. You may return two weeks from today. Now, if you will excuse me, Albret will see you to the gate."

"But, Marchesa, it is with you I wish to negotiate. Is it not true what I hear, that you are, indeed, running this entire seigniory 'like a ship's captain'? A strong woman such as you is certainly able to arrange the marriage of her own daughter if—"

"Good day, Signore Sculli," Costanza interrupted, affronted by his effort to push her to a premature decision. "Marco and I will receive you and your brother Niccolini two weeks hence." Costanza arose abruptly and left, closing the door behind her.

Albret sat on a low window seat in an alcove between the servants' quarters and the kitchens, reading a copy of Virgil's
long narrative poem, *Aeneid*. As the son of a family servant, he
had grown up alongside Bianca at the villa in Rome. Though
Albret was two years her younger, Bianca's father believed it
would benefit his daughter to have the two tutored together in
languages, mathematics, philosophy, and church doctrine.
They became close childhood friends, blurring lines between
mistress and servant. Thus when Bianca married Marco and
Albret moved into the Biliverti castle along with his mother,
he was granted special privileges. Instead of living in the outbuildings or in town as the other vineyard workers and herds-
men did, he was given a small private room in the servants'
area of the castle. At the end of the day's work, Marco allowed
him to read any of his texts from the university as well as
those in the small collection at the castle.

"Good afternoon, Albret. I thought I would find you here,"
said Anabella, taking a seat on a stool near the window. "I see
you haven't finished that Latin epic yet. Why do you find it so
fascinating? My tutor does not insist that I read the classics."
She was dressed in a pale yellow dress with full sleeves, high
neck, and a snug, lace-trimmed bodice. She wore one of the
hairstyles she had learned from Bianca, plaits coiled high at
the back with ringlets falling to the shoulders. Her face was
fresh and radiant and her lips full and rosy.

Albret, though dressed as one of the workers, was handsome with his cleanly shaven face and straight brown locks.
He closed the text and gave the girl his full attention. "I
enjoy reading about Rome, but also the language is so beautiful. I never tire of reading it. I see you have laid aside your
black veil."

"Yes. Sandro's injury and death were a great shock to me,
but life must continue." She sat back and waited for Albret to
make the next statement.

The young man recognized his cue. He felt moved to gush lines of Latin poetry, praising her beauty, then lift the dark ringlet that curled down over her left eye and disentangle it from the longest lashes imaginable. But instead he said, "I have given a good deal of thought, Anabella, to the gash on the back of Sandro's head. We first assumed he had fallen on that nearby rock then rolled over to the position in which you found him. I don't want to alarm you."

"Albret, so much has happened of late. What more could alarm me? Sandro is at peace now, and so am I. Please tell me what you are thinking."

"Do you remember the afternoon I stopped by the infirmary to check on him and you were changing the dressing? It was you who remarked that the wound seemed very straight and regular, not like one made by a jagged rock."

"I recall that, but you made no comment, so I assumed you thought I had made a foolish observation."

"I would never think of you as foolish, Anabella. Strong, adventurous, courageous, but never foolish."

Anabella glowed with the compliment. "Then what do you think?"

"I believe it looked as if it was made by the blunt side of a sword."

"Oh, no. Someone would intentionally hurt dear Sandro?"

"I have wanted to talk further about this with your mother. But she is so overburdened with all the catastrophes of late. . . . When do you think Marco will be back?"

"Mother sent a messenger with a letter calling for his return this very afternoon. Perhaps in a fortnight he will be home. Who do you think struck Sandro?" she insisted.

"That I do not know, but I believe there is mischief afoot. I have inspected the burnt fields and vineyards. I found evidence that the fires were started in various places with stacked brush, drenched in oil. Has your family ever been involved in a vendetta?"

"No, never. My father was a most peace-loving man. Only my half brother has brought dishonor to the Biliverti name, and, as you know, he is no longer a threat. Jacopo was murdered, you know. Do you think the theft of our cattle was connected to this crime, Albret?" Anabella, seldom privy to information concerning events at the castle, was intrigued by the mystery.

"Perhaps. Do not be frightened. Your mother has ordered the hired hands to form a vigil around the clock, posted at all corners of the land. And guards to note all goings and comings at the castle. She has asked me to supervise it all."

"That is good. I will feel secure with you in charge," said Anabella, half closing her eyes with a flutter of those lashes. "Please keep me informed if you learn anything more."

She rose to go.

Albret stood also, as etiquette required.

"Albret, there is something else," she said resolutely, finally mustering enough courage to share her news with him. "Among all the scary things that are happening, there is something really wonderful."

"I would be delighted to hear it, Signorina."

"I may soon be betrothed! His name is Niccolini Sculli. His brother was here this morning and spoke to Mother. Of course she is waiting for Marco to start the negotiations. He is from a very rich and famous noble family in Tuscany. I'm sure he is handsome and charming. Mother is so overprotective. She believes I am too young, but not even the *impalmare* will take place before two years, I am sure. Isn't that exciting? Me, the mistress of a grand castle, and I've hardly filled my *cassone* with a trousseau! Albret, are you hearing? Are you not happy for me?"

Indeed, Albret's face had shown no change of expression. "Anabella, I will always be happy for your happiness. But listen to your wise mother. She may know more about what brings you happiness than you yourself." Albret looked fully at the beautiful maiden before him. Certainly she was no longer the little tomboy in skirts he had found when coming here a year ago. She was blossoming before his very eyes. He was sure she often flirted with him in ever so subtle ways. Often he had fantasized that she actually cared for him.

Anabella puckered her lower lip into a coquettish pout. "Albret, I am not a child." She turned, swirled her skirts, and childishly marched away.

five

Five days following the odd visit of Piero Sculli, Costanza arose early from a fitful night of intermittent sleep and tortured nightmares. Decisions had swirled relentlessly in her mind: Was the offer of betrothal for Anabella a godsend for which she should give thanks, or was it, as her heart told her, born of a sinister intent? Was Anabella's dowry intact, or had Jacopo been able to withdraw it along with the rest of the Biliverti fortune? Was it right to release so many hired workers without consulting Marco? Did the family have enemies as Albret suspected, or were they just experiencing a series of separate misfortunes? Why had Marco not informed her of the drastic state of their financial affairs?

And why had not God intervened? Even though she daily implored Him to rescue her from the disasters in her life, the Supreme Being seemed distant.

After washing and dressing—accompanied by audible sighs—she made her way to the chapel as was her custom. How very alone she felt! She missed Lorenzino with an ache that would not subside. Although her father and Lorenzino himself had arranged the marriage, she had loved him from the beginning. He adored her and provided for her every need. Marco was born the first year, followed by nine years of barrenness before Anabella. Never once did he rebuke her for not bearing him more children. He was good, kind, and wise. Such a man, she knew, was rare indeed. He would know the answers to all that troubled her now. If only he could hold her in his arms. . .

After morning prayers filled with more doubts than faith, she wearily descended the spiral staircase at the front of the castle. As she passed the narrow window on the curved wall, she caught sight of what appeared to be—in the morning fog—three or four galloping horses. She paused. What new circumstance could this be? Slowly she was able to discern a horse-drawn carriage ascending the road that led directly toward the front gate. She watched as the groomsman on guard took the reins of the horses. Who could be calling at such an early hour? None other than Marco and his young wife, Bianca! Costanza gathered her skirts and raced down the stairs, her heart singing with joy.

"Marco! Bianca!" She let the tears flow as she embraced them both inside the heavy front doors.

"Mother dear!" they exclaimed with pleasure equal to hers, but perhaps not with an equal degree of relief.

Their two personal servants brought in all the baggage, and the groomsman took care of the horses and carriage. Albret appeared, from nowhere it seemed, and warmly greeted his mother, Sylvia. He gladly helped her take the bags upstairs.

"Do not tell me you have been all night on the road. There are bandits about and evil lurking everywhere!" exclaimed Costanza.

"No, no, Mother. We did misjudge travel time and arrived in Terni around midnight. We decided to stay at the inn on the outskirts of town rather than awaken you and all the castle."

"I daresay I was awake," said Costanza. "And we now have guards on duty around the clock who could have let you in. But you must not have received my message since you came so soon."

"You sent a message? No, we received nothing, but we should have returned sooner from what—"

"We heard of the fires from the innkeeper," said Bianca, removing her surcoat and bonnet. "The fog obscured the damage as we approached, but it must be terrible."

"Mother, I am so sorry. I should have been here," said Marco, embracing her once again. "I thought I had left all in order, trimming the staff since there would be little to do in the winter months of my absence. I guess I expected the seigniory to run itself with little intervention from you. Disasters always occur when you least expect them. Never again will I leave you so vulnerable." Then he added with a grin, "We also heard a rumor at the inn that you have been directing the operations here like a veritable ship's captain. Could that be true?"

"It is not a role I have chosen, but, yes, I have heard such a rumor, even using those very words." Costanza laughed at this image of her that neither she nor Marco would ever have envisioned until now. "And I have cut the workers again by several, Marco. Most are working as guards. So much has happened. Come, let us break bread in the kitchen. Anabella will be down soon, and there is a matter concerning her—as well as many more issues to discuss."

"We each have exciting news to share also," said Marco as he slid his arm around Bianca's waist and kissed her on the lips with obvious passion. How handsome, young, and full of hope they were!

Costanza pretended not to notice, but the endearing moment reminded her that she too was a woman as well as a "ship's captain." Longings surged, uninvited, through her body. *I will never know such tender passion again,* she thought. *But I am very happy for these two young lovers—and happy they are here at last.*

&

While they ate, Marco confirmed for Costanza that she had made very wise decisions in all matters. As she placed the burdens, one by one, squarely on her son's shoulders, she felt increasing relief for herself. In his keeping, each catastrophe seemed smaller and to have a solution at the end. Soon Anabella joined them around the table. It was a joyful reunion.

&

The next morning, after a breakfast of bread, fruit, and cheese, Anabella followed Bianca eagerly to her studio to see the rolls of completed canvases she had brought back. Many paintings showed the canals of Venice with their gondolas and arched bridges. Anabella was amazed to see streets of water. She begged Bianca to take her to this fairyland someday.

Mother and son turned to Lorenzino's desk to discuss ledgers.

"Yes, Mother, you have correctly interpreted that Jacopo withdrew the entire fortune from the Biliverti account in Rome. That, I am sorry to report, was the larger share. Father, however, kept another account in Florence. See my notation MBF followed by these numbers—"

"That is one thing that worried me," interjected Costanza. "What is MBF?"

"Medici Bank of Florence. Father used the same abbreviation. I tried to employ his methods as much as possible."

"So we retain these holdings?"

"Yes. It still leaves us in difficult circumstances, especially in light of the stolen cattle and the destroyed vineyards. But we are not 'paupers' as you thought. God still watches over us."

"Your father took great pride in his vineyards. They were equal to any in Tuscany and the best by far in the Papal States."

"But we must move on, Mother, and build up what remains to us. At least twenty sheep are to be shorn in the spring. There remain six cows and two bulls. We will have milk and butter after calving season. None of the horses was taken nor the grain to feed them. According to what you have told me, only grass was burned around the old olive trees, and most of the fruit trees were spared also. We have fewer servants and laborers now, thanks to your wise move to dismiss even more. That means fewer salaries to pay and mouths to feed." Marco made all these notations in the ledger.

"Will we not need to hire workers this spring?" Costanza suggested, feeling very much like the business partner she had become.

"Yes, of course. First I must survey the fields and devise a new plan for cultivating and grazing."

"Marco, I could not find any trace of Anabella's dowry in your notations."

"Here it is, Mother: MBF-AD, no change. Which, being interpreted, means there is no change in the size of Anabella's dowry. Actually, there would be a change now. The balance in the state dowry fund earns interest every year, but I must inquire after it. At the time I traveled to Florence to confirm the supplemental account, I was told that Jacopo had attempted to confiscate Anabella's dowry. To withdraw it, however, one must present a betrothal document signed by both parties, a priest, and a notary, which, of course, he did not have."

"I am feeling much relieved. That is one reason I would not allow that Sculli gentleman to see Anabella. I wasn't even sure she still had a dowry. But, Marco, why did you not advise me of our weak financial condition before you left?"

"Mother, I have learned much as a married man. The idea that women should not know too much is pure folly, I have concluded. My Bianca is so wonderfully intelligent. When I consult her about a situation, she is able to help me reason through it. In like manner, it gives me pleasure that you have such interest in business matters. I am delighted you looked at the ledgers, not angry, as you supposed. I only wanted to protect you from unnecessary worry as Father always did. But I see, instead, I have added to your burdens. Forgive me."

"Forgiveness granted," she said with true honesty. "Will you be going back to Padua, or are your studies finished until next winter?"

"I do need to head back in two weeks," said Marco, hardly concealing his excitement. "I have some wonderful news to share with you—a great opportunity that has come my way. But that can wait. I need to check the fields this afternoon while the good weather holds. Do not worry, Mother. I will hire a responsible overseer who can lighten your daily responsibilities. And let us talk further about this marriage proposal for Anabella. We must consider all aspects of such an important decision."

Costanza smiled, feeling a mother's pride in this man-child to whom she had given life, had nursed and trained, and in whom she had instilled Christian virtues. To see him thus—so responsible and wise—gave her great pleasure. Was it not still true that a woman's greatest accomplishment was to produce a good man?

૨**৯**

Marco nudged his horse into a gallop. How invigorating it felt to be home, riding over the hills, even in their charred condition! He had invited Albret to accompany him on his survey of the land. As they approached a fertile slope, they pulled their horses to a halt and dismounted.

"Ah, here's where the choicest vineyard lay. What a shame," Marco said, shaking his head and for the first time feeling real remorse. The good fortune that had recently come his way, as well as the love he felt in his heart for Bianca, veiled his comprehension of the realities his mother had presented to him.

"I will show you where the fires were started," said Albret. "I have not told your mother the extent of this obvious plot. I am also concerned that we may have spies among our workers."

"Spies? Even among the small crew we have left?"

"Of that I cannot be sure. I do not have proof. But I understand you had to hire a mostly new staff when you took charge last year. There is not the loyalty one might expect toward a dynasty such as yours. The two men who lost their lives because of the fire, as you know, were old-timers who had a great influence on the others. They left a moral void where disharmony and jealousy could abound. Trustworthy servants would not let rumors get past our gates. I am certain that has happened."

"I was especially sorry to hear about Sandro. He has been around since I was a child. I remember how pleased he was when little Anabella was born."

"Little Anabella? She imagines herself quite grown up."

"Yes, indeed. And with a suitor already. Do you know anything about this Sculli family, Albret?"

Albret blushed and hesitated. As a loyal servant he must not let his heart color his judgment, but he felt he must say, "Marchese Biliverti, I have inquired of honorable servants in the employ of the two other noble families in Terni. No one seems to know the name. That is not to conclude, of course, that it is not a noble name."

"And did you, by chance, see the gentleman who called?" Marco asked as he dug with a hand spade around the charred stump of a grapevine.

"Yes. Your mother asked that I be in the room as a witness."

"And what did you witness, Albret?"

"Pardon me, Marchese. I do not know if I can give a fair judgment."

"I'm asking you as a young man who has great skill in observation and wisdom beyond your years. Speak out. This is my beloved sister's future we are talking about."

At such urging Albret blurted out, "You must forgive me, Marchese, but I deemed him untrustworthy, without due respect for your sister. He urged your mother to make a quick decision without consulting you."

"Thank you," said Marco without looking up. Then, changing his tone to one of excitement, he urged, "Come—observe this!"

Albret knelt beside him.

"Is this not green wood?" Marco hurriedly dug around the adjacent vine. "These vines are alive, not dead at all."

"Look—here is a sprout already coming from this one!" shouted Albret with equal excitement. "This unseasonable warm weather has stirred the sap. You may eventually have your vineyards back."

"Let's ride out to the other hills and see how widespread this good fortune is," said Marco as he mounted his horse. "And you can show me that evidence of arson of which you spoke."

six

Costanza sat rigidly in a high-backed chair next to Marco, whose relaxed posture announced self-confidence. Across the table the two Sculli brothers unrolled some documents. The red-bearded Piero's appearance had not improved, but Niccolini's doublet, trunk hose, and cape—recently tailored from new cloth—fit his fine shape precisely. His black mustache and short beard were neatly trimmed. Although he remained silent, the young man nervously rubbed his hands together and kept glancing toward the inner hallway where he expected his future bride to emerge at any moment.

The older brother was explaining the terms of the betrothal contract: "In addition to the livestock, our noble Sculli family requests one-third of the Biliverti seigniory so that the signorina may live in comfort not far from her mother." He looked up from the document and smiled broadly at Costanza to emphasize his benevolence. "The Sculli family will build a noble villa for the young couple as soon as they are married. And, as one would expect in these circumstances, we need to be clear in all of which we speak. That being, of course, the full amount of the dowry that will be a central element of the contract."

"That is understood," said Marco.

Costanza gasped at the man's audacity. She and Marco had not come to a decision about this marriage, since both of them had doubts. Was he agreeing to this unfair contract? She knew Anabella, dressed for the occasion, stood by eagerly waiting in the kitchens, with a tray of refreshments in case a servant summoned her.

"Very good indeed, then. We men understand each other."

Piero dipped a quill in ink and offered it to Marco. "Please inscribe the exact amount of the dowry here where it is indicated."

Marco kept his fingers laced together in his lap, which left Piero holding the quill in midair. "I understand a dowry is required, but a portion of the land is out of the question. Besides, the marchesa and I hold other reservations about this merger. Your financial statement seems oddly contrived. We sent a clerk to search the registry of nobility, which includes titles recently granted—and even bought. Our clerk found no such listing of a noble Sculli family in all of Tuscany. There are, however, some inhabitants of the Siena region by that name. I suggest you have overstated the Sculli lineage. Therefore, the Biliverti family respectfully declines this offer of matrimony." Marco and Costanza stood together and bowed slightly as a solid front.

"How dare you go snooping about!" said Piero, raising his voice and taking a firm grip on the hilt of his sword that hung at his waist.

"For my part, I have come to inspect the girl—"

"Shut your mouth, Niccolini," growled Piero. "Come, let us flee from this burnt-out wasteland, this nest of spies!" He marched toward the exit, Niccolini trailing behind him.

Two servants held open the double doors. In the opening Piero turned, raised his sword above his head, and shouted, "The Bilivertis will rue the day they insulted a member of the noble Sculli family. Your total ruin awaits you!"

"And that includes the wench who scorned my proposal!" Niccolini added, narrowing his eyes and spitting out the words.

❧

Anabella, distraught at the news that the marriage proposal had been rejected, slipped to the back of the castle and convinced the guard she needed to go for a short walk to ease her emotional stress. She had watched the arrival of the Sculli carriage from the narrow window on the staircase. With a view of the front gate, she was able to see clearly the face of her intended as he looked upward, scanning the height of the castle. Instantly she was smitten with his handsome figure, noble features, and air of mystery. At thirteen Anabella's thoughts and actions vacillated between mature and childlike. And she herself was the least able to distinguish between them.

How dare Mother make such an important decision about my future without even allowing us to lock eyes, Anabella thought as she marched northward toward the Nera River. "Lock eyes" was a term she had recently read in a romantic tale of knights and ladies.

The clatter of the departing carriage caused her to turn her head toward the road that led from the front of the castle. As she watched, the horses suddenly pulled to a halt. She stood transfixed in the open area, her hooded cape billowing in the breeze. Suddenly the carriage took off again and disappeared in a flurry of dust.

Perhaps Niccolini saw me standing here, waiting for him to return. Perhaps he will come back another day and make a better offer in the negotiations. I know he is the one I love and will love forever. Mother has always overprotected me. I deserve some happiness after all the trauma we've endured. Heavenly Father, please hear my prayer. Following a confident pleading for God's intervention, Anabella turned her steps back toward the castle but with a resolve that led toward an ominous destiny.

&

At the castle Costanza, Marco, and Bianca strolled in the inner courtyard—an intimate little garden of pathways and cultured plants with an inactive fountain at the center. Protected by the castle walls, they enjoyed the warm sun after so many days of chilly weather, their hearts light and happy.

"Anabella seemed displeased with our decision," said Costanza. "Eventually I hope she will understand our reasoning."

"How unlike me she is," said Bianca. "When my parents wanted to betroth me to my father's business associate, I became angry and caused quite a scene. I thought I did not want to marry at all. Eventually, I gave in to their wishes, but Marco rescued me from a disastrous situation. At least she is eager for a betrothal."

Marco took Bianca's hand and smiled lovingly into her upturned face. "Too eager, perhaps," he said. "I want my little sister to have the kind of love we have, and that you and Father had also, Mother. But too much about the Scullis bothers me."

"I am relieved to be rid of them," added Costanza.

"Now that that is settled, Mother, Bianca and I both have some good news to share. Bianca, you may go first."

Bianca's eyes lit up. "As you know, Mother Costanza, I have painted nothing but portraits since I left Rome—except the little scenes of Venice I did for amusement. It is very difficult for a woman artist to be taken seriously and receive the better commissions. But through contacts Marco and I have made in Venice, a committee from the church of San Cassiano has requested I do a rather large altarpiece. To think it will be hung in the same church as a masterpiece by Il Tintoretto!"

"That is wonderful, Bianca," responded Costanza. "I am so happy that your talent is recognized."

"We both feel this is a great opportunity for her. It will bring her recognition and will enhance her reputation. I am very proud of my wife," said Marco. "Now for my good news. Mother, you recall how I have raved over my teacher Galileo Galilei. He is the one who requires us to use experimentation rather than memorize by rote."

"Yes, you were assisting him with some device to enlarge the appearance of objects at a distance, I believe."

"That is the one. Well, last month he turned this instrument, called a telescope, toward the heavens. At last he is able to refute the claims of Aristotle that everything in the heavens is perfectly round and smooth. Is not that amazing?"

"Yes, amazing!" Costanza echoed her son's enthusiasm but without fully comprehending.

"I too have looked through this telescope at the moon and can plainly see it is covered with mountains and valleys, very much as is our earth. Now he is seeking to prove that Copernicus was correct in believing that the earth and planets rotate around the sun. The earth may not be the fixed center of the universe!"

"Marco, you frighten me!" gasped Costanza. "Such ideas may be unpopular or even condemned. Are you sure you wish to be associated with a man who has such radical theories?"

"Do not worry, Mother. The duke of Tuscany in Florence has already shown great interest. Galileo is writing a book he will call *Sidereus Nuncius,* about his observations of the heavens. He has asked me to assist him in his experiments as well as in writing the book. He believes his findings must be made public as quickly as possible ahead of other scientists and to limit official criticism. I think he will be one of the greatest men of all time—and I will be at his side."

"That is truly wonderful. But, Marco, what of our plight here at the seigniory?"

"My work with Galileo should be complete by mid-March. Then I will be here through spring and summer and until after the harvest in fall. The notary we used to keep on staff has agreed to be on call. He will look over the books once a fortnight. Also, in my absence, I have asked Albret to be our overseer. He is a very bright young man. Among the books I brought him is one on mathematics and record keeping. He can keep the daily records with the occasional help of our notary. He will have a key to Father's study, with your permission, of course."

"Yes, I do trust him. But he is so young—"

"He will soon be eighteen. Since he is tall and muscular and naturally tends to speak with authority, I believe the men will follow his direction. They already think of him as a scholar."

"I can attest to his honesty and dependability," added Bianca. "We grew up together almost like siblings, taking lessons together. He was my private guard the last year I was in Rome."

Costanza surmised that the two of them had privately discussed the plan to make Albret overseer.

"Mother, you have already appointed a new chef to replace Sandro. He is working out well. You will be in charge of the rest of the domestic staff. If another suitor shows up, you can request that he return in the spring. I see no rush in having our 'Bella betrothed. She should have another year, at least, with her tutor; don't you agree?"

"You are right on all counts, Marco."

As Marco set everything in order for another departure, a sudden thought struck him. He smiled. "Mother, have you ever considered marriage again for yourself?"

Costanza blushed, obviously embarrassed at such an idea. She raised one eyebrow at her son in the same manner she had often done when he was a small child. The message was clear: *You have stepped across a line.*

Marco accepted the admonition and returned to the business at hand. "Can you think of anything else I can provide for you before our departure?"

"I am sure I can handle everything now," she said as though he had never strayed from the topic. "Surely we have seen the end of bad circumstances for awhile. You have provided me with more than ample money to run the household. I presume Albret is sufficiently supplied for his duties."

"Yes, of course."

"I do feel so much more secure now that we are not totally destitute, as I thought. The vineyards will be back in a few years. All is well."

Costanza left the young couple to stroll down the path toward the center fountain, hand in hand. She retreated to her favorite window seat where a basket of wool yarn awaited. She had started a shawl intended for a woman who begged at the church door. As she sat clicking the needles at a furious pace, her tangled emotions wove themselves into the yarn. The love so evident between her son and her daughter-in-law emphasized her own emptiness and kept her loss ever before her. *Their relationship is so strange,* she thought. *Marco keeps nothing from his wife. He seems to make no effort, as Lorenzino did for me, to shield her from the worries of business and the stress of decisions. Yet Marco tries to do this for me. Still, I must take on responsibilities out of necessity, unfamiliar and uncomfortable as it may be. And what did Marco mean by "considering marriage again"? Does he suppose another fine Lorenzino will come riding up to my gate in a horse-drawn carriage? A quaint idea indeed!*

⁊⬝

But in the following few days the family enjoyed together, laughing, sharing stories, and indulging in the new chef's delicacies, they easily forgot the threat pronounced by Piero Sculli at his departure: *Your total ruin awaits you!* Anabella remained sullen, hardly speaking until the day of Marco and Bianca's departure.

On that day she became delightfully talkative and animated. Finally, catching her brother alone, she grabbed him by the sleeve and pulled him into the inner courtyard. "Marco, may I have a private word with you?"

"How lovely you look this morning, dear 'Bella," he responded, following her out into the garden. "It's good to see you once again in high spirits."

"Marco, listen to me. You have been saying how a woman should express her thoughts. That she need not always adhere to a man's decisions."

"I am not sure I have put it in those words. I certainly listen to what Bianca suggests to me—"

"I, as a woman too, suggest that I wish to be betrothed to Niccolini Sculli. Where are you going to find another such as he? The two titled families in Terni have no young men. We are so isolated here, and Mother is too protective. This may be my only chance at marriage—the most worthy of any woman's pursuits. Do you not agree?" She cocked her head and pouted her lip.

"I agree it is a worthy pursuit, but, dear sister, I can find many contacts in Venice or Padua if I look. It is only that, well, frankly, I had thought of you as a child. You are not a child; that I can see."

"Will you implore Mother for me? She listens to all you say," Anabella pleaded.

"Anabella, no," he said, placing his hands on her shoulders and looking directly into her eyes. "I do not wish more burdens put on our mother. She and I agree that Niccolini Sculli is not worthy of you. You must accept our decision." He lifted her chin in his hand. "I will, however, make inquiries of families I know in Venice before I return in the spring. That is a promise. We will talk further about this matter at that time. Until then, keep up your studies, help your mother, and don't cause her any worry."

"Yes, Marco," she said and bent her head.

So anxious was he to return to Padua that he failed to take note of her petulance.

seven

Five men sat around a table at the Bardi Inn halfway between Terni and Siena. The weather had turned cold, and they had just finished a hot meal of lamb stew. They were laughing uproariously at each other's jokes. Piero, the oldest, ordered another bottle of wine.

"We have a vendetta to craft," he growled in a low voice as he filled a goblet for each man. "I thought surely after the fire and the loss of cattle that the Biliverti woman would be primed to go for the betrothal. Perhaps demanding land at this point overstepped—" All guffawed heartily as though he were telling another tale.

"We should have waited, but no matter. Eventually the whole seigniory will be ours," said Ugo, one of the two middle brothers. "We will not stop until it is." He lowered his voice and repeated a story the brothers knew by heart. "Jacopo Biliverti cheated us out of what was rightfully ours. King Philip's soldiers paid him well for ridding the Spanish government of its enemies."

"But the gold belonged to all of us who had a part," interjected Niccolini.

"Jacopo has paid dearly, but not dearly enough. He promised we would be living in luxury along with him as soon as he became master of the castle."

"And that never happened."

"But it will! We will establish the Sculli dynasty on the ashes of the Biliverti land," declared Piero as he pounded his fist on the table.

Anslo listened intently. He was not a member of the Sculli clan and had to play his hand shrewdly. He recalled the rumors about the night Marco had fled for his life from the castle. They said Jacopo, who had failed to entice Marco to drink the poisoned wine, sent a posse after him. Rather than join the pursuit, Jacopo rode out alone, half-crazed over his failure to do his half brother in. According to rumor, he was killed by bandits for the small bag of gold he had with him. *That's what these men mean by "Jacopo paid dearly." They murdered him for revenge!* thought Anslo, putting the pieces together.

"We couldn't get our fortune by marriage"—Piero emptied his glass and wiped his beard with his sleeve—"so we will win it in ransom!"

"Aye, aye," the brothers agreed and lifted their goblets. The levity stopped suddenly, and all became somber.

"Here's the plan," confided Piero. The men leaned in, their heads close together. "Anslo, you must keep close watch on all the activities around the castle. That's what we pay you for. That Marco has gone again, which leaves us with only women-folk to deal with."

Together they schemed and plotted the details.

❧

Anabella, reputed to be a pious and obedient girl, fought with the extremes of emotion so peculiar to adolescence. Her entire being was focused on her desire to become betrothed to Niccolini Sculli. She could concentrate on nothing else and neglected her studies accordingly. Somehow she must devise a logical and practical plan to present to her mother—perhaps to host a ball. Then, after the plans were set, she could casually suggest adding her gentleman to the guest list. Mother had neglected their social life since Lorenzino's death. They used to have such grand parties in the ballroom.

She would love to discuss the matter with Albret. In his presence she felt a tingling of excitement—not unlike the feelings that came over her when she imagined locking eyes with Niccolini. But in his new capacity as overseer he seemed somewhat aloof. Besides, he took her mother's side when

Anabella had broached the subject before.

The guard at the north side of the castle seemed to defer to her wishes of late. Ever since the cattle had been stolen, her mother had ordered the guards to keep a log of persons entering and leaving. Mostly this was to keep track of the servants, but the order also was intended as protection for Anabella.

The girl knew she was never to leave unaccompanied, but this particular guard would usually wink and say, "Don't be gone long, Signorina. You must not bring worry to your mother." She peeked at the log and saw that her name had never been recorded. Thus, since it had become so easy to disobey, she slipped out each afternoon at a time she knew her mother was preoccupied. Hiking over the hills or through the wooded area gave her a sense of freedom and allowed her to think on her favorite subject uninterrupted.

Today she escaped later than usual. Her mother, needlework in hand, had insisted on sitting beside her at the little pupil's desk to ensure she did the sums assigned by her tutor. Afterward her mother read aloud a letter from Marco in which he had written volumes about his wonderful science instructor, Galileo, and the experiments he was doing. Anabella, although she adored her brother, became bored and agitated. Finally her mother left to supervise the cheese making.

Outdoors she ran toward the woods that had been spared in the fire. She had brought a basket in which she hoped to gather vines, leaves, and pine cones to craft a wreath for amusement. At the time she left the gate, after exchanging pleasantries with the guard, the day had been warm with sunlight streaming through the gathering clouds. She had worn a light cloak, gray in color, over a dark blue dress, her tresses tied back with a dark ribbon.

As Anabella strolled along the path, poking here and there with a long stick she had found, the skies darkened. Wind suddenly whipped through the trees, and the first drops of impending rain stung her face. Startled, she pulled her cloak about her and shivered. Visions of Niccolini shattered. She turned and headed toward home, leaning against the force of the wind.

Lightning crackled; thunder clapped. Without warning, a large black cloth fell over her head and shoulders, and arms of steel crushed around her body. She heard her own muffled scream.

Sometime later, she awoke to the realization that she was riding a galloping horse. Rain poured down. The soaked cloth over her head lay plastered against her face, making breathing difficult. She tried to move her arms and felt ropes binding them to her body. A man's arms reached around her to hold the reins of the steed. She could hear the hooves of another horse ahead as they sloshed through the downpour. Terrified beyond hope, she clenched her fists. *Lord Jesus, save me,* she prayed. *I have been a disobedient and willful child. Forgive me. Forgive me. My punishment is death. I feel it. Death or worse. Worse? No. Dear Lord Jesus, protect me from worse than death.*

It seemed as if they rode thus for hours. Her body rigid and her eyes squeezed shut, she repeated her prayer over and over. Eventually the rain subsided. The horses slowed and trotted side by side. Tree branches scraped across her head. For the first time, she heard the voices of her captors.

"How's our little prize?" scoffed the man on the adjacent horse.

"She feels good to me." The man behind her pulled her even closer and laughed.

Anabella knew she was helpless in his grasp. She could not so much as move her hands to protect herself. Dread and panic gripped her.

The man clasped the reins again, and the two returned to single file as they wove slowly through the brush. Finally they halted.

"We'll set up camp here for the night." The man dismounted and unloaded her like a sack of flour. He set her on a large, smooth rock, removed the ropes, and pulled off the cloth. Then he bound her hands behind her back. Water streamed from her drenched hair and into her eyes. She blinked continuously.

The rain had stopped, but the darkness was complete. She could hear the men moving about, unloading gear, and talking in low tones. She caught only a word now and then. She heard the sound of an ax chopping, as if on dead wood, then on saplings. She heard flint strike against steel. When the flame shot up, she watched one of the men light a lantern. She could now see his face as he held up the light. This man, at least, was unknown to her. The voices hadn't sounded familiar, but still she wondered if they had targeted her specifically or merely picked her at random.

His partner emerged from the darkness with a load of wood, dumping it only a few steps from her. He took dry sticks from his saddlebags, stacked them next to the damp wood, and lit them with fire from the lantern. Anabella watched every move with apprehension. Fortunately, they ignored her as they went about setting up a tent over the sapling poles and roasting goat's meat over the fire.

When the meat was roasted to their satisfaction, one man, whose voice she now realized was the one behind her on the horse, held a bone with meat to her mouth. She shook her head. "Now don't go starving on me, Anabella," he said. "We promised to deliver you in perfect shape."

"And a perfect shape she does have," laughed the other, reaching out his hand to grab at her.

"No, no! She's not to be touched. You know the orders." This from the one who had held her on the horse. "Here, Wench, eat!" He shoved the meat at her again. Again she turned away.

So they do know me. But who are they? And why me? Thoughts raced through her head.

"Bedtime, my sweet one!"

"You gonna keep us warm tonight?"

"We'll put her between us, Ugo. We can share, can't we?" They both laughed.

The one called Ugo pulled her into the tent. By the lantern, she could see three pallets, two side by side and one across the entrance. That formation dispelled the fear that she would be between them. Ugo retied her hands, this time in front, gave her some leeway and attached the other end of the rope to the tent pole next to one of the pallets. The man pushed her down, ran his hand over her body, snorted, and left. She sat upright in terror. In total darkness and despair, she dared not move.

Mercifully, her captors intended to sit around the fire and drink awhile. At first she paid no attention to the droning of their voices punctuated with guffaws. Then she recalled something her tutor often said: *To know is to have power.* She must listen closely.

"You gave the ransom note to the guard?"

"And paid him generously. No problem there. Anslo arranged everything."

The guard? And Anslo? Why would Anslo want to kidnap me? Thoughts swirled around in her head. That scene at the river flashed across her mind. She had told no one about that revolting incident, too ashamed to let anyone know. Least of all her mother. *Oh, Mother, you must be crazy with fear by now. How angry you must be toward me, and rightly so. I thought I was so clever sneaking out. I thought I knew so much. I know nothing, nothing at all.* She shook her head and trembled, but no tears came.

". . .Niccolini. . ."

Niccolini? She strained her ears to put words together. How could Niccolini be part of this? Surely it was another Niccolini. It was a common name.

". . .rise of the Sculli name and. . ."

Now there was no doubt! Niccolini Sculli! Love boiled into hot anger. It surged through her body, turned to resolve, then renewed energy. She tore at the bonds around her wrists with her teeth until she tasted blood. To no avail. The ropes were wet and taut. She felt along the short leash until she found the knot around the tent pole. She ripped at it with her nails, then her teeth. It began to loosen. Freedom at last!

No. Her two captors sat outside the opening. She must wait for an opportune moment. With that thought, she loosely retied the end of the rope to the pole, turned toward the side of the tent, and lay still. She prayed over and over again for direction. For God to intervene. For rescue. A calmness settled over her, and she fell asleep.

≈

A startling crash broke her rest. Another crash. Frightened neighing of horses. A clatter of hooves. Cursing.

Anabella sat up. *The horses have been spooked by the thunder and torn loose from their tethers, and the men have chased after them,* she concluded.

"Thank You, Lord," she whispered and untied herself. She slipped out of the tent into more blackness. She could hear the men in the distance, yelling. She walked gingerly at first, reaching out a tentative foot to feel her way through the brush. She held her bound hands in front of her to protect her face. But her captors would soon discover her escape and pursue her. She increased her pace, allowing the branches to tear at her arms and face.

The heavens opened and drenched her without mercy. She trudged on through the rain, often stumbling, sometimes falling. Hours passed. Somewhere she lost a shoe. Her hair fell in dripping strings about her face. With no idea of her whereabouts, she tried to stay in a straight line, hoping it would lead someplace. Again she prayed for God to lead her to safety.

The rain let up. A flash of lightning gave her light for one brief moment. In front of her stretched a wide road, muddy and full of ruts, but a road that led somewhere. She stood transfixed, not knowing which direction to choose. Again she placed her life in God's hands. She turned and followed the road to the right.

eight

As soon as Costanza discovered Anabella missing at the evening meal, she mobilized all the employees and servants and divided them into search parties. Although greatly worried, she dealt efficiently with this new calamity. She knew her daughter's adventurous spirit and believed the blame lay mainly with her. Her worry, then, was tinged with annoyance.

She guessed her daughter had made some excuse to one of the castle guards—perhaps an innocent-sounding request to gather parsley from the gardens or some such. But the log showed no record. Under scrutiny, all the guards claimed to know nothing of her departure. Obviously, she was nowhere in the castle for it had been searched and searched again.

A staircase stood on the inside of the east enclosure, but from the top of the stone wall one would then have to jump three meters to the ground below. Not dangerous, however, for an agile child who could scoot on her stomach, feet first, across the top of the wall then drop. Costanza accepted this route as the most plausible.

Under questioning, Anslo admitted seeing her strolling about the estate on various past occasions but had thought nothing of it. "A girl her age has a mind of her own, she does, even if it's to her detriment."

As the storm broke and darkness began to fall, Costanza's worry turned to distress and finally to despair. With only two guards at the castle and Clarice, her personal maid, wringing her hands, Costanza was left desolate and inconsolable. She paced the empty halls and silent rooms. She stopped at the chapel and pled with God to return her daughter, her only daughter, the one she loved with all her heart.

She sat on a window seat at the end of a hallway, holding a candle and staring out into the darkness as rain lashed unrelentingly against the castle and a bare branch scratched like a giant skeleton hand against the pane. Footsteps echoed up the staircase, preceded by the light of a torch. Costanza turned, both frightened and hopeful.

It was the guard from the north gate. He stood, in all formality, before her. With a slight bow he handed her an envelope that dripped with rainwater.

"What is this?"

"I found it tied to the north gatepost, Signora. It is sealed; therefore I know not its contents." He bowed again and waited for instruction.

Costanza broke the seal and tore the contents from the envelope. After reading it, she dropped the paper in her lap, covered her face with her hands, and wept in loud laments. Clarice came running and put her hands around her shoulders in an attempt to comfort.

"How may I be of service?" the guard inquired, standing at perfect attention.

After a few more sobs, Costanza gained control of herself. "Please, when Albret returns, send him to me immediately. You may go."

❧

Within the hour Albret dashed up the staircase, carrying a lantern in one hand and some object in the other. Costanza, still sitting at the window seat, looked up.

"Signora, please excuse me, but I have found something that may belong to Anabella." He approached Costanza and held the object between his lantern and her candle. His hand trembled with concern for Anabella, the one he cared so much for.

Costanza reached for the long strip of narrow cloth and took it in her hand, damp and muddy though it was. "Anabella's hair ribbon. This is the dark blue ribbon she was wearing today. Oh, my baby, my precious baby."

"I found it in the woods."

Costanza sobbed into her handkerchief, blew her nose, and spoke in the calculating tone she had learned to use for business matters. "Albret, she has been kidnapped. They want ransom money—an amount almost equal to her dowry. We do not have nearly enough scudi here at the castle. The note is not signed. Look—here is where we are to leave the bags of gold." She pointed to the instruction on the note. "Come—let us go to the study and decide a course of action."

&

A train of three carriages, a horse-drawn wagon, and several pack mules made their way slowly over a muddy road. The sun broke through streaks of red and gold clouds that spread across the eastern sky. The barone, Antonio Turati, leaned out the window of the lead carriage and sang at the top of his rich baritone voice, *"Le dis–gra–zie non ven–go–no mal so–le."* He breathed in the crisp air and turned to his aide, Paolo, and said, "Ah, 'tis a beautiful morning. Troubles may come and go, but we should savor the delicious moments when they are ours."

"Yes, Signore, like our good fortune to arrive at the farmhouse last night at the onset of the storm. Always, it seems, people are standing ready to befriend you."

"The farmer was paid well. Actually a delightful family. I always enjoy playing with the children. Each time I stop, they seem to have one more bambino than the time before—"

Paolo interrupted to point to a waif standing beside the road. "Signore, what could a child be doing out here alone, so far from a village?"

"Beggars are everywhere. Hand me that half-loaf on top of the bundles."

Antonio took the bread and held it out at arm's length as he passed by. *"Dio vi benedica!"* he shouted.

Anabella turned her mud-streaked face up to his and took the gift in her bound hands without looking at it. She spoke no words, but her round eyes expressed both fear and helplessness.

"Stop the carriage!" Antonio called to his driver. He waved a flag out the window, signaling the rest of the train to draw to a halt.

Antonio jumped to the ground and walked back to the child. He stood before her, hands on hips.

"I see you are a girl," he said gently. "Where could you have spent the night? There is not so much as a hut in view."

Anabella clutched the bread to her chest and stared back at the stranger. "I do not know where I am," she said simply, then crumpled into a heap at the barone's feet.

nine

Costanza did not even go to her bedroom. Instead she paced and prayed throughout the night. Often she revisited the window seat at the end of the hall, even though nothing could be seen through the rain. This morning she sat on the little balcony overlooking the front gate. She watched the sun rise over the hills, the dawn of a new day, and sighed. *Can Anabella see this new day, wherever she may be? Does she live?*

Albret and two guards were already on their way to the notary who was to accompany them to Florence to withdraw the money for ransom. She had signed a paper with her instruction. There would be little left after she bought her daughter back. Anabella's dowry could not be withdrawn without a betrothal document. According to law, if Anabella were to die, the investment in the state dowry fund would go to the city. Poverty again knocked at the Biliverti door.

Noon found Costanza still sitting on the balcony. Clarice had brought her a cape and insisted she take some nourishment. She nibbled a biscuit and sipped the hot herb drink her maid had prepared. Waiting was most difficult. She could not expect the return of Albret and the guards for two or three days. Yet looking down the road helped her feel involved. The half-knitted shawl lay untouched in her lap.

Suddenly, galloping horses emerged from behind the hill and headed up the road toward the castle. Costanza stood and leaned over the stone railing to get a better look. As the horsemen drew nearer, she was able to recognize Albret, followed by the two guards. She ran down the stairs. Why would they be returning so soon? Was Anabella dead? Had they found her body? She burst through the heavy front doors and clattered across the flagstones and through the wrought-iron gate the guardsman held open for her.

Albret jumped off his horse and ran toward her, shouting, "Anabella is found!"

Costanza threw her arms around his neck and kissed him soundly on the cheek. "Where is she? Is she all right?"

"Yes and yes," answered the young man, his cheeks flushed with excitement. "She is in the lead carriage coming around the hill." He pointed in the direction.

Costanza stared in disbelief as the string of vehicles and mules came into view. "That is a merchandising train. You left my Anabella with a miserable merchant!" she gasped.

"No, no. It was the 'miserable merchant' who found her," explained Albret. "We met them on the road, and he, a Signore Turati from Florence, stopped us to ask if we could identify an exhausted girl who slept on the backseat of his carriage."

"And it was Anabella!" Costanza sobbed tears of joy. "This is a miracle sent straight from heaven! Praises be to God, our protector!"

The guard summoned groomsmen who would stand ready to care for the horses and mules when they arrived. Costanza wanted to run to meet the carriage but waited patiently by the front gate.

When the lead carriage finally pulled in, Anabella was sitting up. Her hands were free, and she had sponged the grime from her face. A woolen blanket had replaced her damp cape. But scratches, bruises, and hollow black circles around her eyes told a horror story that broke her mother's heart.

She emerged from the carriage and bowed her head before her mother. "I have done wrong, Mother. Can you ever forgive me?" she whispered in a barely audible voice.

Costanza and Albret supported her from either side, as she appeared too weak to stand alone.

"Anabella, God has given you to me twice. Once at birth and now returned from the dead. Whatever has happened,

God has forgiven you as have I."

Antonio stood awkwardly next to his carriage. "She did not tell us much. So—her name is Anabella? Well, I am happy to have found her home. We will be on our way as soon as the animals are refreshed." He turned to step up into his carriage.

Albret and Costanza had already passed through the gate toward the castle, completely ignoring everything else around, so absorbed were they in the returned Anabella.

Costanza suddenly realized she had not thanked the medium of this wonderful miracle. She stopped and called back over her shoulder, "Signore, I am grateful to you beyond measure. You and all your men must come inside and refresh yourselves. Our chef will prepare something for all to eat. How many are with you?"

"Twenty-four, Marchesa Biliverti, but. . ."

"All of you will stay the night. I insist." At the doorway Costanza turned around and faced the merchant. "Please, Signore, I must tend to my daughter. Our guardsman will care for your needs and see that the chef prepares something for everyone. I will return shortly." She turned toward the castle.

Albret carried the girl, a cold and damp burden, up the stairs. Yet Costanza noted his joy mixed with pain, a reflection of her own emotions. He looked into Anabella's pale, wan face. Her eyes were closed, and her full lips parted slightly. After placing her gently on her bed, he returned to his official duties and prepared for the reception of the group.

Clarice and Costanza removed Anabella's still-wet clothing and bathed and dressed her in a fresh nightgown.

"I will bring you some hot soup and bread," the mother said soothingly as she tucked her child in bed.

"No, not now, please. The barone gave me some bread," Anabella said and pulled the blankets up under her chin. "I walked all night in the rain. I am so tired. . . ." Saying that, she closed her eyes and fell asleep.

Costanza kissed her daughter's forehead, smiled with

thanksgiving, and left for her own bedroom. She knelt at the window and thanked God for answering her prayers. A sense of comfort surrounded her, and she believed she felt the very presence of God. Anabella had revealed enough for her to know that, horrible as the experience was, she had not been ravished.

She raised her eyes and saw a little embroidered sampler Anabella had made for her a few years back. Framed in violets, the stitched words declared: *Nihil solliciti sitis sed in omni oratione et obsecratione cum gratiarum actione petitiones vestrae innotescant apud Deum et pax Dei quae exsuperat omnem sensum custodiat corda vestra et intellegentias vestras in Christo Jesu.* She whispered the meaning in the vernacular: "In every thing by prayer and supplication with thanksgiving let your requests be made known unto God. And the peace of God, which passeth all understanding, shall keep your hearts and minds through Christ Jesus—Philippians 4:6–7." She remembered that Anabella had chosen the verse from an inscription in one of the church's chapels. Now it seemed to speak through her daughter to her heart in a new and meaningful way.

As the peace of God settled over her, she was able to turn toward the reality at hand. The person who had rescued her daughter waited below as her guest. She freshened herself from the bowl of water on the stand and coiled her hair into a bun, high at the back of her head, and left a fringe of ringlets to frame her face. Over the bun she placed a small coif. Taking a cape of dark green silk, she draped it over her shoulders and clasped it with a jeweled brooch. Indeed, she portrayed all the elegance fitting her station.

☙

With Clarice at her side, she entered the reception room where she expected to find her guest. Instead a younger man, clean shaven and well dressed, stood waiting. With a bow he said, "I am Paolo, principal aide to the barone. Your overseer, Albret, has seen to it that all the men have been served in the servants' dining area. They are now storing our merchandise from the mules' backs in a safe area he has indicated. I trust this is as you would wish, Marchesa Biliverti?"

"Yes, exactly, but. . ."

"Ah, the chef suggested that the barone and I lunch at the little table in the inner courtyard. A most charming spot, Marchesa. It must be even more lovely with flowers in the springtime."

"Thank you. Is the barone. . .?"

"Signore Turati."

"Yes. And where is Signore Turati?

"In the kitchens, Signora."

Costanza stood with her mouth agape.

At that moment the barone entered. Costanza turned to face a tall, broad-shouldered man who possessed an air of majesty. His dress expressed the very latest fashions in Rome. She noted the gold embroidery of his black velvet doublet and the intricate designs etched on the sheath of his dress sword. The traces of gray in his wavy sideburns and narrow mustache did not extend to his fashionable *pique de vant*—a short, pointed, black beard. Most of all, the twinkle in his eyes delighted her.

To her surprise he carried a tray, holding a silver carafe and four porcelain drinking cups from her own cabinets. "So the lost is now found. Let us celebrate. I offer a small gift for our hostess, the Marchesa Biliverti." He set the tray on a side table. "The coffee, that is. I took the liberty of using utensils from your kitchens and borrowed these wares. I left the bag of coffee for your use, Signora. Please sit down, and I will serve you."

Costanza did as she was bid, astonished at the man's unusual actions. She wondered how he knew her name. Albret must have told him.

He poured a cup for her and one for himself. Paolo, apparently accustomed to his master's habits, took the tray to the other side of the room and poured for himself and Clarice.

"Have you yet tried this new drink, Marchesa?"

"Only once at an affair at the neighboring villa. It seemed very bitter." She sipped the drink. "But this is quite good—sweet and creamy, Signore Turati."

"Yes, I made it as they do in Rome. It is called *caffelatte* and is quite the fashionable trend there," the man said proudly. "And you may call me Antonio."

"As you wish—Antonio," she said with some hesitancy. "For that matter, I prefer signora to marchesa. I am widowed. Thus my son is the current marchese, and I defer to my daughter-in-law as the marchesa. It is less complicated that way."

"Would Costanza be too intimate? I ask because I certainly do not wish to offend my generous hostess."

Costanza could feel heat rising to her cheeks. No man had called her by her given name since Lorenzino. "No," she stammered. "I mean yes—yes, that would be perfectly satisfactory."

The social banter became serious when Antonio said, "And how is Anabella? I do hope the girl will not be ill. I do not know what has happened to her or why she was out there all alone. Did you know her hands were bound when I found her?"

"I guessed as much when I bathed her wrists. I must admit that I had despaired of ever seeing her alive again." Costanza covered her eyes with a lace handkerchief and blotted the tears. "Please forgive me. I am so relieved to have her back under this roof. She is my only daughter—I treasure her so."

"Of course you do. Children are very precious." An uneasy silence hung between them for several minutes. Each was lost in a private reverie: Costanza indulged in joyous scenes of her daughter's childhood; Antonio held a small boy who was no more.

"My Anabella was kidnapped for ransom," Costanza said abruptly. "I struggle trying to figure out who it could have been and why. She will eventually tell me what happened, but all I know now is that two men abducted her and tied her up. She says they did not hurt her. Thanks be to God! And she escaped in the rain, in the darkness, and walked all night long. All night in the rain and darkness."

"Poor child," whispered Antonio.

Another awkward silence ensued. "Perhaps your overseer would be so kind as to give me a tour of the premises. Later, Costanza, you might enjoy looking over some of my merchandise. I have wonderful, finely tooled leather goods and every sort of savory cheese imaginable."

Costanza, shocked by the man's boldness and reference to business, found herself at a loss for words. Here was a complete stranger asking to look around the estate. He could have an ulterior motive. Even a dashing barone could be a spy. And, of course, a merchant would want to take advantage of this unique opportunity—to sell goods to a poor widow in a weakened frame of mind. *Ah,* she recalled, *we still have the money I would have paid for the ransom. Again we have been snatched from the jaws of poverty.*

"Forgive me, Costanza. I did not mean to intrude. I am always interested in the layout and structuring of an estate. From the expression on your face, I discern a reluctance. . ."

"Yes, Signore," admitted Costanza. "I keep a close guard on the property. With reason. Please understand."

Antonio finished the contents of his porcelain cup, set it on the saucer, and leaned toward Costanza. "I understand fully, Costanza. You are a very strong woman to know when to refuse a request. I admire that."

"One does what one must," said Costanza, somewhat coolly. *Who is this man who calls me Costanza so easily—is outrageously bold, yet gracious?*

"To you I am unknown, Costanza," he said in answer to her silent question. "But I often did business with your husband, Lorenzino. An astute businessman he was. He always selected the finest bolts of wool and silk. He had an eye for superior porcelain also. I daresay, he purchased these cups from me several years ago." He looked into her startled eyes.

Costanza's distress came from conflicting emotions. In one way she felt invaded. This man, who had gone into her kitchens uninvited and used her porcelain ware, now claimed to have once owned it. He had known her husband. The material she had cut and sewn, embroidered—with which she had clothed her family—had come from this man. Somehow she resented being told all this. Yet he was charming in his boldness, and there was comfort in knowing he had sat in this very room, negotiating with dear Lorenzino.

"I see I have blundered, Signora. I did not intend to upset you. Frankly, I am not in the habit of talking to women such as you—especially a woman distressed. Please accept my apology. Thank you for your generous hospitality, but we will be on our way. We can make it to Perugia by tonight if we pack up and leave immediately." He and Paolo rose in unison.

"Signore—Antonio, no," said Costanza, softening her brow. "Albret will show you and Paolo the estate. I have already ordered the chef to arrange for a gala dinner this evening. I am sure they have slain a goat and are preparing pasta at this very moment. This is an emotional day for me. You have stirred even more emotions in recalling my dear Lorenzino."

"If you are sure, Costanza," he said. "I do not wish to impose. You see, I am in the process of building a villa and laying out my estate near Florence. I take great interest in such things."

ten

While Antonio's clerks and others in his entourage were being served in another area, he and Paolo dined with Costanza and Albret, clustered around one end of a long banquet table. Since Albret had been elevated to the lofty position of overseer, Costanza had chosen him as her male representative from the castle. A tall and ornate candelabra shed light over the little group. Two male and two female servants brought the various courses in an efficient manner. Throughout the sumptuous meal, the men discussed politics, the popular artists in Florence and Rome, and new scientific discoveries.

Costanza remained silent as women were expected to do. In fact, the men ignored her presence. As an avid reader of Marco's university texts, Albret was eager to display his knowledge. Paolo, an almost constant companion of Antonio, was equally well versed.

Antonio, though modestly spoken, appeared to know a great deal about everything. He also seemed to be a friend of the poet Giambattista Marini, who had been imprisoned for his satires of those in high places. And he had met and dined with Claudio Monteverdi, writer of operas.

"Have you, perchance, heard of the great discoveries Galileo is claiming to have made?" asked Albret.

"Is he not amazing?" responded Antonio enthusiastically. "I have heard he claims the large star Jupiter has four planets of its own that rotate about it. I tend to believe he is correct."

"He must have made the discovery with the telescope he has been pointing toward the heavens," Costanza said suddenly, motioning to the servants to clear the plates from the table. "I understand he has detected mountains and valleys on the surface of the moon."

The three men stared at her in astonishment.

She sensed that they saw her as impertinent as she had thought her guest bold that afternoon. "He seeks to prove Copernicus correct in believing that the sun, not the earth, is the center of the universe and that the planets, including our earth, rotate around it."

"I am amazed at your knowledge—but delighted," stammered Antonio. He seemed puzzled by the woman's entering uninvited into male conversation. "So you are interested in science?"

"I tend to believe that Galileo is correct in his findings," she said, not directly answering his question. After all, she was only quoting a few statements she had heard from Marco. Indeed, she could not have continued the conversation in depth.

"And where, may I ask, have you. . .?"

"My son knows Galileo personally. He assists him at the University of Padua." Why not do a little bragging of her own?

"That would be Marco, I presume."

Now it was Costanza's turn to be thrown off balance. *Not only has he known Lorenzino, but he knows Marco also.* She had not meant to be rude by breaking into the conversation, but she had grown fatigued with listening to these men engage in intellectual sparring. She had listened happily hundreds of times, sitting next to Lorenzino. Back then she was part of him, and thus he spoke for both of them. Tonight she had felt invisible in the silent role.

"How can you possibly know Marco?" she asked in a softer tone.

"He was present, Costanza, with your late husband the last time I was at this castle, selling merchandise." He also spoke in a gentle, less boastful, tone. "I wish to thank you for this delicious banquet, Costanza, and again for your hospitality in lodging my entire troop tonight."

All stood. Servants brought night candles for each person

and started to snuff out the flames of the candelabra.

"Wait," said Antonio. "We will need the light." Paolo and Albret expressed their gratitude for the evening, bowed, and left for their rooms.

"Come, Costanza—I will show you how caffelatte is made. In Rome, one enjoys a cup to cap the end of a fine dinner."

This man is overpowering, thought Costanza. *And I should not go into the kitchens with him. That would be unseemly. Of course he is married. How could such a handsome, gifted, and intriguing man not be?*

"I am widowed, like you," said Antonio as though he had read her thoughts. He carried the towering candelabra like a torch of triumph toward the kitchens. What could she do but follow?

❧

The kitchen help bustled about finishing their cleaning and storing. The fire in the largest oven had died down to glowing coals—a perfect spot to boil water and heat milk for the special drink.

Antonio and Costanza sat on tall stools at a high table in the corner of the spacious kitchen. "Now that you have taught our chef as well as me how to make this delicious drink, I will, no doubt, indulge rather frequently," said Costanza, setting down her empty cup. "But I am surprised you are so comfortable in using kitchen utensils."

"Even though I keep a staff at both my town house in Rome and at the country villa I am finishing near Florence, I often prepare my own meals. I arrive and leave at odd hours." He smiled at Costanza, looking directly into her eyes. "You are fortunate to have a child still with you. Children make a hut or a castle a home, I believe. And how is Anabella faring?"

A shadow passed over Costanza's countenance. With difficulty, she suppressed her anger over Anabella's kidnapping. "It is difficult to tell," she said politely. "She has developed a fever and complains of chills. But she finally took some soup this afternoon and fell asleep again before I came down to dinner—poor, exhausted dear. Clarice is sitting by her bed with instructions to fetch me if she wakes."

"A sick child can be a great concern," said Antonio. "A few times I have brought a street urchin to my place. I provide him care for a few weeks until he is in better health. Then, as I have many connections in both cities, I arrange for an apprenticeship for him. A few years back I brought a nine-year-old boy along on a merchandising trip. He was delightful and a great help to me. But a traveling life is not for one so young. I taught him arithmetic, and he now keeps the accounting books for an establishment in Rome."

"What a good heart you have!" exclaimed Costanza. "You must have a great faith in God to be so giving."

"Someone took me in off the streets when I was nine. I am but returning the favor. No, I would not say I have a great faith in God. I believe He is up there. I think He is on the side of good. But I do not know if it makes much difference to Him what I do. If He has the power, why does He not rid the world of all the evil and heartaches?" He wrinkled his brow and shook his head.

Costanza was stunned, but touched, at Antonio's openness. "I wish I could answer that, Antonio, but I do not know the answer myself. For me, at least, it seems that I find a nearness to God in the midst of heartache and trouble. After Lorenzino died, my children and I went to Rome. We were going to stay a week or so with my brother there. Jacopo, Lorenzino's son from his first marriage, confiscated the castle and prevented our return for a year. Marco—such a good son!—worked as a stonecutter. Anabella and I sold our needlework in the market. We also found a church and studied Scripture together and helped the poor and needy. I must say we had very little ourselves, but I felt a peace and happiness in helping others." She hoped her words would encourage this good man to continue his search for the source of his goodness.

"I had heard you begged on the streets of Rome. I am happy to hear that is not so," he said, recalling the rumor Julius had passed on to him.

"All sorts of false rumors were flying about at that time. No, we were never forced to beg. The church found us a place to live. Then Jacopo—God rest his soul—was murdered by bandits. We took up again our noble life here which, until recently, has been comfortable. My faith is firm, but sometimes God does seem distant.

"Like you, I am grieved at suffering, especially when I see beggars in front of the church. I take food and clothing to distribute every Sunday when we go to the church of San Salvatore. My husband always felt we were doing a great service in the world by hiring so many of the townspeople. But I am sure you noticed the burned vineyards when you toured the estate. Most of our cattle were recently stolen. Therefore, we have had to let over half of our workers go. There will be no harvest next fall."

"And do you believe God knows or cares about these things?"

"What I believe is that when we pray to God with a sincere heart, He hears us. We may not always receive what we ask, but He has promised a peace that is more comforting than understanding. I felt that peace today when you brought Anabella back to me. I felt the same peace in Rome even though God had not spared my dear husband's life. Yes, I believe God knows and cares."

"Perhaps someday I will be as certain as you. I would like to be."

The kitchen crew began leaving, having finished their duties. Both Costanza and Antonio knew it was late, but neither felt inclined to leave. The sharing of their lives brought an intimacy that neither had known for a long time. The coffee they had just consumed also had no small part in their lingering.

"So you are actually acquainted with Monteverdi? Is it not he who is combining theater and music into a form of entertainment called opera?" Costanza grasped at this idea to prolong the evening.

"Ah, yes, he is the first to breathe life and passion into such performances," he said, seeming eager to accept her invitation to linger. "Costanza, wait here a moment."

He slipped into the hallway and returned with the lute he had left standing against the wall. Settling again on the high stool, he began strumming. From Monteverdi's latest opera, *Arianna,* he intoned the deserted lady's lament: *"Lasciate mi morire. . ."*

Costanza listened enraptured. An entire orchestra and cast could not have been more thrilling. He sang heartily with richness of voice and feeling. Following a couple of Italian folk songs, he ended with a tune about "my darling," *amore mio!* Costanza wondered if the words were meant for her, hidden in the guise of a song, but dismissed the thought.

"Alas, it must be past midnight," Antonio said, setting his lute down. "We must pack our mules and leave early on the morrow." He cupped his hand under her elbow and helped her down from the stool. They walked side by side to the staircase and turned toward each other. Each held a candle which shed glowing light on their faces.

"Buona notte," said Antonio awkwardly.

She was surprised when she sensed within herself a yearning for him to take her in his arms, but she knew a gentleman would dare not do so.

"Buona notte."

Costanza found her daughter fast asleep. She sat beside her awhile and prayed that her evil kidnappers were far away and would never return to harm her loved one again. With so little information, it would be difficult to apprehend them.

Then, putting her anguish aside, she crept to her own room. Once in bed she lay on her back, eyes wide open, and allowed herself to relive and savor every moment she had spent with Antonio Turati. *I think I will buy some leather boots, in my size, before Antonio leaves in the morning!*

In his room Antonio knelt by his bed—although it was not his custom—and prayed to God. *Thank You for the gift of this evening. It must have come from You, for I could not have planned it. I do believe, but help my unbelief.*

eleven

A large, stone farmhouse sat isolated on the outskirts of Siena. The grounds surrounding it remained unkempt, and dead vines obliterated the windows. Rain pounded on the ancient tiles of the roof, and wind whipped around the corners, rattling the loose shutters. Inside, one might be startled at the strange conglomeration of sparse furnishings—the rich and ornate Spanish tapestries; the frayed, brocade Renaissance couch shoved against the outer wall of an alcove. Four men sat on benches that surrounded a great freestanding hearth where a fire flickered eerily. The alcove, attached to the central kitchen, formed a sequestered meeting place for the Sculli brothers. Upstairs their elderly mother, the wives of the three older siblings, and their children slept, for it was far into the night.

"Foiled again!" hissed Piero as he raised a clenched fist. "How could you have let that wench get away? Answer me that, Ugo and Tristano." He sat back and poured himself another goblet of wine.

"Excuse me, esteemed brother, but if you had not been so greedy in forging a marriage alliance, we would never have needed. . ."

At that Piero let forth a string of curses. "My actions are no basis for your excuses! We must assess our options and plot our next move if our insults are to be avenged. For that matter, the refusal of betrothal only furnishes another insult that must be confronted to protect the sacred honor of the Sculli clan. A shrewd move on my part, would you not agree to that?" He grinned broadly at his own cleverness.

"Yes, of course," said the three.

"Tell me this," Piero growled, as his reddened eyes darted

back and forth between the two brothers. "Did the wench ever know you were Scullis?"

"No, no," Tristano assured him. "We had that cloth tied over 'er head until it was dark. Then Ugo lashed 'er to the tent. It was black as tar, it was, that night. I think she was in a trance or something. We discussed nothing in her hearing—I'm sure of that. Somehow she got out while we chased our runaway horses in the thunderstorm. She might be dead by now for all we know."

"They didn't deliver the ransom money at the time we set. Niccolini and I gave them time to draw from a bank. She must have gotten home. When do you meet with Anslo again?"

"Sunday after next," said Ugo. "He's got the whole day off. Me and Tristano will meet him at the Bardi Inn as usual. He can make the entire trip in a day if he gets an early start."

"I don't trust that Anslo. He's not of our family blood," said Piero. "But we need him. You say there's a new overseer he keeps his eye on?"

"Some upstart kid, Anslo says."

"We need to compose our revenge narrative," said Piero abruptly. "Tristano, you have the best hand. I'll tell you what to write."

"Why do we need to write it down?" asked Niccolini, sounding like an unmotivated scholar. Piero frowned to let him know the question was not a worthy one.

Tristano quickly gathered writing supplies. Piero dictated: "Be it known that this day, 15 of February, 1610, the Brothers Sculli set forth a vendetta against the family Biliverti, seeking just compensation, first, for the injury done by Jacopo Biliverti in withholding funds owed to us. And second, for the insults to our honor by Marco Biliverti in rejecting, as unworthy, our pure intent to merge two great families in the marriage of Anabella Biliverti to our esteemed Niccolini. As Jacopo no longer lives, his debt to us must be born by his brother, Marco, being next of blood kin."

"Bravo!" exclaimed Ugo. "The following generations of our family will be proud we did not flinch, that we did not go down in shame, but honorably fought for just revenge."

"That's good, Ugo. Write that down, Tristano."

Tristano did as he was told.

"Our mad blood stirred us to outrage! We cut those Bilivertis to pieces! Blood flowed every. . ."

"No, no. Don't write that down. Niccolini, this is to be a proud document. We seek only what is rightfully ours. After all, if authorities demand an explanation for our deeds, we have this written document to show. They will know we only acted honorably to right wrongs against us."

Niccolini lowered his handsome head and sulked.

"The authorities do not look all that favorably on vendettas today," cautioned Tristano. "We must avoid prosecution, at all cost. We could, perchance, offer a duel? The conflict is regulated, following precise rules."

"Excellent, Tristano. And you are the best of us with the sword," said Piero.

"I accept the challenge with honor."

"Marco's refusal to fight would bring shame to his family. He could not possibly decline," said Ugo.

"Yet storming the castle would be grander. We can easily stir up a small army and pay them off with some of the loot," offered Niccolini, ready to rejoin his brothers in plotting.

"And how many castles have you stormed, little brother?" scoffed Tristano.

"The last one, when all we gained was that worn couch over there. But I did my share of scaring the women out of their wits."

"That you did, Niccolini," Piero said with contempt. "Whatever approach we take, this must be done cautiously. We cannot afford more blunders. Vendettas are still recognized as legitimate, if we show good reason. The worst the authorities in the Papal States would do is banish us to our own region here in Tuscany."

The brothers argued, plotted, and schemed, spurred on by drink, until early morning. The next day they spent snoring in their beds, dreaming visions of themselves as conquering heroes, avenging wrongs.

ॐ

Rain continued daily for two weeks. Anabella's fever increased, and at times she grew delirious. Costanza stayed by her bedside, bathing her face with cool, damp cloths. Although gifted in care of the sick and dying, Costanza found nursing her own daughter increasingly painful. She blamed herself for not being more diligent and for not warning the girl more forcefully of the dangers that lurked outside the castle—and especially among men.

In short periods of time, while Anabella slept, Costanza would slip downstairs to the kitchens and make herself a carafe of *caffelatte*. Making it as Antonio had shown her and sipping it atop a high stool somehow brought back some of the pleasantness of their short time together. The morning of his departure she detained him as long as she dared in selecting items to purchase. Albret helped her choose harnesses and other leather goods needed at the stables. She bought a bolt of coarse wool for the servants to make outer garments. And finally a pair of leather boots for herself. She would need to tramp around the estate to keep her eye on activities and make decisions regarding planting. She might even take up riding again.

Today she held a cup of coffee as she sat at the window in Anabella's room. She watched the rain stream down in little rivulets outside the pane. The last words Antonio spoke to her echoed in her mind: *We will see each other again, Costanza.* He had held her hands in his and looked down into her upturned face. *My business brings me through Terni from time to time. Until we are together once again, God be with you.* He had squeezed her hands lightly, let go, then swung up into his carriage without looking back. The carriage had moved forward with the packed mule train following. She tried to recall her own words but could not. Perhaps she had said nothing and only stared back at him like a stunned doe. She could remember standing at the front gate, watching the train until it turned at the curve in the road and disappeared behind the hill.

What did he mean by saying we will see each other again? He will come by to sell us merchandise once or twice a year? Or did he mean he would purposely come to see me again? Maybe soon. Surely he sings to many women between Rome and Paris. And many he promises to see again. She sighed heavily.

"Mother, are you there?" Anabella sat up, startled to see her mother in her room. "Are you all right?"

"Anabella, yes, yes, my sweet. You are the one not well. Or are you?" Costanza rushed to lay her hand on her daughter's brow. "You are no longer feverish! Are you feeling better?"

"How long have I been ill? The days and nights are mixed together in my head. Yes, I think I am better, but I do crave some cool water."

ða

Anabella improved quickly. Finally the rains stopped, and the sun dried the standing puddles. Costanza eagerly awaited Sunday so they might go together and thank the Lord for His goodness. She enjoyed worshipping in the ancient round church of San Salvadore, built in the fifth century by the Romans. Somehow when she looked up into the large dome, she felt connected to the thousands of Christians who had prayed through the centuries to the same eternal God as she. Her heart was full of praise, and she rejoiced in Anabella's recovery. She would also thank God for the time spent with Antonio and for her renewed faith.

Anabella's return to health brought with it a maturity and wisdom. She showed a special sensitivity to her mother's needs and a willingness to accept her protection.

·❧·

As always, beggars stood at the door of the church as Costanza and Anabella stepped from their carriage. Clarice and her husband, Pico, as well as Albret, accompanied them. Costanza brought the shawl she had knitted for the poor woman she saw so often, but today she searched through the ragged group without finding her. A child held out his hand. She placed a coin in it and asked if he had seen a woman of her description.

"Signora, I think she died two weeks ago," he said.

"I am so sorry to hear that," she said as she placed the shawl in his hands. "Here is a blanket to keep you from the cold at night." She was grieved that she had not done more and done it sooner. With so much suffering, one could never do all that was needed.

"Thank you, thank you, Signora," the boy said, burying his face in the clean-smelling wool. A young man, with scars of burns on one side of his face, placed his hand on the boy's shoulder.

"Thank you, Signora Biliverti," he said.

"Mother!" exclaimed Anabella. "This is one of the workers who helped fight the fires." She turned to him. "I remember you were helping fill the vats of water, but then you decided they needed you at the vineyards."

"I am sorry," Costanza said. "I did not recognize you. Do you have more family?" She had never been out among the workers until that awful night, but now she recalled treating his burned face with olive oil in her infirmary.

"My wife is at our hut with our baby girl. My older son has just found an apprenticeship with a shoemaker. He is inside the church as he has no need to beg, thanks be to God. Please forgive me for mentioning this, but I have not been able to find work since. . ."

"Signore—"

"Massetti."

"Signore Massetti," said Costanza, "you and this boy come

in with us. We will worship beside your son as you no longer have need to beg, either. As of this moment you are rehired. Report at the castle gates in the morning, and ask the guard to speak to Albret, this young man beside me. Spring will arrive shortly with all the work of cultivating and planting. At last there is much to be done."

As the man was thanking her for her generosity, a lady of high rank, on the arm of her husband, approached.

"Signora Biliverti, I hoped I would see you today. We have missed you the past two weeks. I hope you have not been ill."

"No, but Anabella has not been well."

"Good morning, Signore and Signora Bargerino," said Anabella politely. "As you can see, I am in robust health at this moment and eager to praise God for His delivery."

"That I can see. And a lovely young lady you are, my dear. I have brought this invitation to Carnaval for your family today. I do hope Marco and Bianca will be here for the festivities. It will be a small gathering at our castle, as last year—just the three noble families of Terni, a few cousins, and other guests. Is this young gentleman with you?"

"Yes, this is Albret Amaseo. He is our new overseer."

"I see. Then you, Signore, are invited also. We hope to have several young men and ladies."

Costanza assured the Bargerinos she would let them know of her intentions in good time. The Massettis had already entered the church. She did not want them to think she had deserted them for better company and thus was anxious to terminate the conversation.

Last year she had declined the invitation to Carnaval and stayed home, feeling uncomfortable without an escort. Also she had thought Anabella too young for such festivities. Marco and Bianca, however, had found it extremely entertaining and said she should have ventured forth. This year Costanza felt more self-confident. She might bring Antonio—if only in her heart.

twelve

As Anabella grew stronger, she resumed her studies, meeting with her tutor twice weekly. She returned to her household chores of helping the kitchen crew, mending, and making articles for her *cassone*—in case she were ever betrothed. Costanza felt she also needed fresh air, and now that the rains had passed and the days were warmer, she proposed a carriage ride for her daughter.

At the end of their usual breakfast in the kitchen, Costanza said, "Anabella, I have asked Albret to take time off from his duties this morning to accompany you on a ride over the estate. That way he can also check the road conditions after the rain, and you will benefit from the air. Clarice will go as a chaperone."

"A chaperone? Mother, Albret is all the protection I need. He is very adept with his sword. I have seen him practice."

Costanza smiled. "But, my dear daughter, he is a man. And you practically a woman. Sparks can ignite under the most benign conditions."

"Yes, Mother. I have learned that you are much wiser than I," said Anabella in true sincerity. "By the way, I hope you have accepted the invitation to the Carnaval party at the Bargerinos. I have not danced since—since I was a child."

"I know—I have sadly neglected our social life. It would be so much easier if Marco and Bianca were here. But I do not expect them until mid-March."

"You and Father were always the center of festivities. People would crowd around you waiting for Father to say something witty. I was always so proud to be your daughter. It must be difficult to go to social gatherings without him."

"Yes. You have a great deal of insight, my daughter. But

now I must compose my own witty remarks. What would you say to that?"

"You? Speaking out? I cannot imagine it. But why not? Bianca speaks out all the time, and Marco beams with pride."

They both laughed. Anabella found it amusing to picture her mother speaking out with a crowd enthralled with her. And Costanza recalled the scene at the banquet table when three men had stared at her for her impertinence.

❧

Anabella sat up front next to Albret who held the reins. Clarice happily sat behind them in the open carriage, free from duties other than keeping an eye on the young couple who bore all the decorum necessary. Anabella wore a cocky, black velvet riding hat, tilted on the side of her head, and a black surcoat over a blue embroidered dress with upstanding collar. Long coils of curls hung to her shoulders. Albret was dressed as a gentleman in new doublet and hose, ordered by Costanza after his recent appointment. His hat, like Anabella's, was made of black velvet but trimmed with a fine feather.

Grass was already turning green, effacing the charred stubble. Sunshine and blue skies announced the approach of spring.

"Let us stop here a minute," said Albret as they arrived at what used to be the choice vineyards. He jumped out with a little spade he had brought along for this purpose and dug around the burned-off vines, going from one to another. He stood and shook his head.

"What is it?" asked Anabella.

He returned to the carriage and methodically wiped the mud from his hands with his handkerchief. "The vines did not survive the rains and cold. Earlier, during that warm spell, Marco and I found the wood green at the roots and even some sprouts coming up. Now they have rotted."

"Mother will be so disappointed."

"Poor lady. She has had more than her share of heartaches,"

said Clarice, shaking her head.

They rode along in silence for some time. This was the first Anabella had heard that the vines might come back. Often she felt left out of what was going on around her. This would certainly be another blow to her mother.

Finally she turned to her companion. "I love being out-of-doors, Albret. Actually, I envy you spending so much time out here."

"Yes, I enjoy it. At first, when I became overseer, your mother expected me to do all the accounting of the ledgers in the study. I did not mind doing it, but I spent far more time than I liked indoors."

"But I see Mother taking more time than you in the study as of late."

"Yes, she insisted I show her methods of accounting, and she has been studying the mathematics book Marco left for me. Your mother is an amazing woman, Anabella. I have never heard of a woman wanting to keep books before." The two chatted away, at ease with one another, as they bumped over the dried ruts in the road.

"She is so much wiser than I thought. I should have obeyed her when she forbade me to leave the castle alone. The world can be a wicked place."

"Anabella, your mother was not the only one who grieved over your disappearance. I thought my heart would break when I found your hair ribbon in the woods." Anabella noticed an anguished expression pass over his face as he recalled that night.

"It was truly a horrible experience." She turned toward their chaperone. "Clarice, would it be permissible for us to stop awhile and sit on the rocks over there in the sun? I have been indoors for far too long."

"Of course—I'll sit up front and hold the reins. Just stay in my view," the servant said. She had no reason not to trust these two.

Albret stopped the carriage, jumped to the ground, and ran to the other side in time to assist the young lady in her descent. He took her hand to help her climb the rocky path to some large, flat rocks. They sat down a reasonable distance from each other and faced the carriage that held the watchful Clarice.

Anabella thrilled at the brief touch of Albret's hand. She could have climbed rocky paths all day like this, though that was not to be. *He has been so aloof of late, but he is not at all aloof today. And he thought his heart would break when he found my ribbon?*

"Would you like to tell me what happened, Anabella?"

She began the narrative at the beginning and left out nothing—except for the times Ugo touched her. "Lying there in the tent, wet and cold, I listened to their conversation around the campfire. They mentioned ransom, so I knew I had been kidnapped for that purpose. Then I heard them mention the name of Niccolini Sculli. The men evidently had been sent by him. This is no way to acquire a bride, I would say."

Albret paled visibly at the name Niccolini, but he kept his composure. "I agree with that. What I do not understand is why he would think he could get away with it."

"I suppose I have a large dowry. Maybe he thought if he—you know, if he—if I—spent the night with him, then my family would have to agree to the marriage." She struggled with the words but at the same time needed to share at least some of the horror she kept bound within her.

"Knowing your mother, I believe she would have taken you back. Though Marco might have challenged him to a duel."

"A duel over me? No, I would not want that. Marco might be killed."

"He is quite adroit with a sword. We have fenced together several times, and I consider myself rather good. I was well taught by Bianca's father so that I could defend her if necessary. Marco usually won, however. But, I agree, dueling is no better than a vendetta in settling a dispute."

"There is something else, Albret. Because of the horror, I have forgotten a lot of the experience, but recently something has come back to me. I hesitate to tell Mother because I do not wish to worry her further."

"Yes, Anabella? Go on."

"I overheard one of them say Anslo had arranged everything. That he had paid the guard generously. I cannot figure out how Anslo would be involved with Niccolini."

"Anslo? That man seems always to be around, whatever I am doing. I do not think he likes me; yet, if he has no specific task, he is lurking somewhere near me. I told Marco I thought spies were among the workers, but I had no proof. It seemed strange to me that gossip about the Bilivertis spread so quickly through the town. Of course, all would know about the fires, but bits of conversations I had heard here seemed to find their way to the public. For example, I heard one of the workers admiringly say your mother directed the fighting of the fire like a ship's captain. Then, when Piero Sculli came to propose your betrothal, he chided your mother for not making a decision, as he had heard she ran this place like a 'ship's captain.' "

"Anslo probably heard the same remark by the worker as you. He then passed it on to the Scullis." Distress mounted in her voice. "Albret, I was so foolish to think I loved Niccolini. I know now that such feelings are meaningless."

"Not meaningless, Anabella—misplaced." He smiled knowingly at her. "You will have such feelings again, I am sure. But it is hoped that they will grow out of friendship."

Is he saying our friendship could grow into true love? I do not think so. I never again want to trust such emotion, she thought. But aloud she said, "Albret, I hope never to be betrothed. If it had not been for what I thought was love, I never would have disobeyed Mother and slipped out alone."

Albret chose not to argue. "Anabella, let us keep our eyes open to all that goes on around this castle and seigniory.

Perhaps the Scullis have more in mind than a betrothal. Remember our little discussion in the alcove when we talked about how Sandro's death had not looked accidental? You wondered if his death, the fires, and the cattle were all connected. I think you are right. I will see to it that the guard in question is dismissed, but I want to find out more of what Anslo is doing before I approach Marco or your mother. What do you think?"

"What do I think?" Anabella, unused to having her opinion sought, hesitated before answering. "Yes, I think we both need to look and listen for clues. We know Anslo has some part in this, so we must be wary of him. Also I believe all the guards need scrutiny. Perhaps others are being paid. It makes me feel insecure again."

"I do not want you to be insecure. Stay indoors, unless accompanied, and always be alert. You are quite right. I will check the credentials of the other guards." He looked into Anabella's trusting face and silently vowed in the future to protect her always from harm. Never had she appeared more beautiful. And never had any woman possessed such long and tantalizing eyelashes.

thirteen

Costanza sat at the desk in the study, poring over the numbers. She had come to enjoy working on the ledgers, recording everything bought or sold, subtracting, adding, placing the numbers in the correct columns. At first it had been difficult, for she had forgotten much of her lessons learned as a child.

But the more she understood the methods and practiced arithmetic, the more fascinating it became. Since she wrote more neatly and precisely than Albret, it was easy to convince him to bring her his scribbled notes, and she would make the final entries.

Today, however, she frowned as she made calculations for the future. The remnant of the Biliverti wealth in the bank could last only about five years if nothing more was added. That wealth had been built on the vineyards that produced choice wines sought after all across Italy. Not only had Albret informed her that the roots of those vines had rotted, but he said he had talked with other vine growers. They told him that even if the vines sprouted up again, they would probably produce only wild grapes. She must find new sources of income. If she managed well, the seigniory could support not only the Bilivertis for generations to come, but she could also hire back the workers who had lost their means of support. *I will find a way,* she declared. She closed the ledger and retired to her room to dress for the Carnaval festival.

❧

The past week Costanza had hurried the restoration of the old wedding carriage. Heat from the fires had blistered the paint. Hard use had left cracked wood and a broken spoke. Now it was finished. The baroque carvings were freshly gilded, and four elegant horses, wearing new leather harnesses, pulled it along the road to the neighboring Bargerino castle. Pico held the reins, and Albret, dressed as the gentleman he was becoming, perched beside him on the elevated driver's seat. Inside the curtained coach, along with Clarice, sat Costanza and Anabella, facing two guards who suffered the ladies' skirts to flair across their shins.

Anabella adjusted her black eye mask, which she wore for the first time ever. All women of rank donned them at both public and private events—partly to conceal their identity, but mostly to be fashionable. It added an air of mystery. Both ladies carried feathered fans of ostrich tips. The mother had instructed the daughter on proper etiquette: how to hold the fan, not to remove the mask, to speak only to those to whom she had been introduced.

Albret turned to Pico and said in a low voice, "I think a group of men is following us at a distance on horseback. Slow down and see if they slow."

"There is a tree limb in the road ahead. I'll stop and remove it. That will give me a chance at a good look."

He did so, but when he climbed back in the driver's seat, he said, "I believe you are imagining things, Albret. I could see no one." Both men knew the importance of staying alert to danger.

They arrived safely at dusk, alighted from the carriage at the front gate, and entered the magical world of Carnaval. In Rome, festivities had been in progress since the sixth of January with parades, tournaments, jousting, and entertainment of all sorts. The Bilivertis had always preferred the more intimate gatherings in protected castles among friends they knew. Tonight was the last night before putting away the meat and commencing the Lenten season. Danger lurked in every corner in the large cities, and even in Terni people had to be constantly on the alert for bandits. But inside the castle a trusted butler confirmed the identity of each guest.

They entered a large ballroom where perhaps fifty people

milled about engaged in conversation. The multiple-candled sconces along the walls shed soft light on large oil paintings, their frames encrusted with gilded scrolls and shells. Streamers of colored ribbons hung from garlands of greenery over the arched passageways. Costanza and Anabella were acquainted with most of those present, but Albret knew no one. Signora Bargerino made the introductions. Pico and Clarice found their counterparts in another room, and a guard shadowed each of the ladies throughout the evening.

Various entertainers performed in different parts of the room and even down a wide, lighted hallway. A young man sat on a chair in one corner simultaneously playing a pipe and a tabor, the drum slung over his left wrist and kept in position by his knee. On a miniature stage Pulcinello, the puppet, performed on the hand of a young girl who spoke for three characters in as many voices. Down the hall, the young people could take turns challenging the last winner of cup and ball.

Anabella flitted from one station to the next, talking vivaciously with any whose name or face she recognized. Indeed, many eyes took note of this lovely creature. A pudgy boy her own age tagged behind her, asking every question imaginable to keep her attention. He soon lost out, however, to a Bargerino cousin from Siena in his twenties, who joked about her hiding her eyelashes behind her mask. Anabella ignored him completely, as she had been instructed, until he said, "Anabella, do you not remember me from three summers ago when we danced at your castle? I am Frederigo."

"Ah, yes, Frederigo. I did not recognize you with a beard."

"You were a mere child then. Now, I daresay, you are the most beautiful signorina at this ball—even with your lashes hidden—and I claim the very first dance."

"As you wish," said Anabella with a blushing smile.

At that moment, various stringed instruments struck up a lively tune, and Frederigo swirled her off to the center of the ballroom.

Anabella glanced over her shoulder to see Albret withdrawn into a darkened corner, standing awkwardly with arms folded. His timidity in this social arena amused her. She was so used to seeing him comfortable in his intellectual pursuits and self-confident as he supervised others.

Costanza sat at a small table with two other masked ladies whose husbands were gaily dancing with their female kin. They talked of grown children who forgot their manners, of needlework, of lazy servants, and of the depressing rains that had finally passed. Costanza, bored beyond numbness, finally brought up a new topic.

"What do you think are the best crops to grow on the rocky hills of our region?"

Both women stared at her with mouths open. Certainly this was not a subject for female conversation.

"I mean besides our wonderful grapes."

"Will not your son, Marco, make such decisions?" said one, realizing it was a sincere question.

"Yes, of course, but I am interested in—in agriculture." She dare not mention that Marco was absent from the castle.

"Well," said the same lady, "since I have no say in the matter, I have never thought much on the subject."

"Nor I," said the other. "But I overheard my husband say that wheat was a good crop. 'There are always markets,' he said, 'if you can get a merchant to pass by here to sell it in the cities.' Or, if you want to start a silk-processing industry, you could plant mulberry bushes."

"The mulberries would grow well on hillsides, do you not think?" probed Costanza.

"I do not think at all," said the first lady. The two gentlewomen smiled at each other and agitated their fans.

The dance ended, and both husbands approached to sweep away their wives.

"Wait," said the second lady to her husband. "Costanza has some questions about wheat and mulberries. Why not have this dance with her?"

"Delighted, Costanza. You should not sit here alone." She took hold of the man's arm and let him lead her to the floor. "We were all sorry to hear that your vineyards burned. So Marco is looking for a new crop, is he?" She soon learned that wheat was an excellent crop for the region, but it should be planted on level ground. Mulberries could easily replace the grapevines on the hillsides, but the industry of producing silk was quite complex.

Now that someone had offered an initial dance to the attractive widow, others followed suit. The men who had known and admired Lorenzino hesitated to step into his place. But when they saw how charming and witty she was on her own, they eagerly awaited a turn. For Costanza's part, she imagined that each partner was Antonio Turati.

Anabella, equally charming and witty, never missed a dance. She savored every moment of the attention lavished upon her and forgot about Albret. Forgot, that is, until she noticed that he no longer stood alone in his corner but with a rosy-cheeked young maiden who chatted away, touching his arm every few seconds for emphasis. Anabella entertained the thought of asking him to dance with her, but, alas, it was time to enter the dining hall for an extravagant meal.

All were in a jovial mood as they filed into an area where two long parallel tables, lit by multiple candelabra, awaited them. The gentlemen sat on one side of each table, the ladies on the other. Anabella was directed to sit next to her mother on the outer side of one table, whereas Albret sat facing her but at the other table. And directly across from him she could see the bobbing curls of the rosy-cheeked maiden.

Following the first course, basins of rose water were brought for finger dipping. A youth with a viola strolled between the garlanded tables and sang love verses in Latin. *Albret should enjoy these Latin verses,* thought Anabella. *He can understand the words.* She dared look across at that youthful, ruddy face and caught him gazing across at her. Immediately he lowered his eyes.

Next a mountain of game birds—peacocks and pheasants—arrived on huge platters, carried on the shoulders of two servants. Then capons in parsley sauce, roasted eel, and almond soup served to the sound of voices from a boys' choir. Another hand washing, this time in lemon-scented water.

Finally, marzipan and a variety of sugared fruits were served, accompanied by a reading of a comic poem written by Lorenzo de' Medici about hunting with a falcon. During the hunt everything went wrong, and the hunters decided to go fishing instead. Everyone laughed. To end the evening, all stood and sang a doxology in praise of the Lord who provided such bounty.

Farewells and gracious thanks were expressed to the hosts, Signore and Signora Bargerino, for a marvelous celebration. Frederigo sought out Anabella, took her hand in his, and asked that she remember him next time her family hosted a ball. She agreed politely, but secretly she regretted not having danced with Albret. *I could have taught him how. He need not have been so shy,* she thought. She searched in vain for the curly-headed girl, but at least she was not near Albret.

Pico brought the carriage to the front gate where the Biliverti party boarded and left in haste, as it was well past midnight. Inside the coach, Costanza eagerly listened to Anabella's version of the evening, pleased that it had met and surpassed her expectations.

"And, Mother, I noticed both men and women sought your company. I saw those ladies gasping at your witty remarks," Anabella teased.

Costanza smiled. "Perhaps we were discussing the planting of wheat and the raising of mulberries."

Anabella frowned, then assumed this to be a joke and laughed heartily.

On the driver's plank, the conversation turned to weightier matters.

"Albret, one of the workers who was let go is now in the employ of the Bargerinos. He pulled me aside and told me a horrible story. You remember that during the fire Sandro fell and later died from a head wound," said Pico.

"Yes, go on."

"This man overheard a conversation between Sandro and Anslo. He was sitting down behind the wagon, resting for a minute. They didn't know he was there. Sandro said he was sure the fires were set on purpose because they were so widespread. Anslo said he had better not spread such lies around if he valued his life. They continued to argue. He could hear some scuffling. They went back into the brush. He heard a thud. After awhile Anslo returned and saw the other worker. 'We'd better get these vats filled up,' Anslo told him. 'They're going to need more water.' At about that time Anabella came up, he said, carrying two buckets of water from the river. That girl should never have gone out there."

"So he thinks Anslo killed Sandro?"

"He didn't say that exactly, but I'm sure that's what he thinks."

In the moonlight Albret noticed the outlines of four or five men on horseback at the top of the hill nearest the castle. "Do you see that, Pico?" He pointed upward. The figures turned their horses and disappeared behind the hill. "They plan to ambush us as we come around the curve in the road. Leave the road and go behind the hill on the left. Perhaps we can get past them before they spy us."

Pico followed his advice. Albret glanced quickly at the interior of the coach, concerned that the ladies would be alarmed. They appeared drowsy from the late hour and the swaying of the vehicle, unaware of the change in direction. But the guards sat up straight, alert to whatever might be amiss.

This was a much longer route, but when they emerged from behind the hill, they could see shadows waiting past the large rocks. "Swing wide so they do not hear us," directed Albret.

"We are behind them since they are facing back down the road."

"Too late! Here they come!"

Pico lashed his whip out over the horses and urged them to a gallop. The horsemen were gaining. Costanza and Anabella clutched each other in panic. Clarice covered her face with her hands.

"We are being chased by bandits!" said one of the guards.

"There should be a torch holder with an oil-soaked cloth inside, right under your seat," said Costanza to the guard. "Quick! Light it from the lantern and throw it out the window!"

"Brilliant!" said the guard and did as he was told.

Albret turned to see the flaming torch fly through the air toward the men. The horses reared and neighed in fright. The riders lost control long enough for the carriage to arrive safely at the castle gate where groomsmen waited. The three ladies jumped unassisted from the coach and ran past the gate, across the flagstones, and through the double doors, held open by the castle guards.

Pico and Albret rushed to mount saddle horses and set out after the bandits in hot pursuit. The torch that had successfully frightened the horses lay extinguished in the dust. After a few miles they drew to a halt and listened.

"Not a sound," whispered Albret. "They've gone to seek other prey."

≈

The five men, after gaining command of their horses, had fled into the woods and watched Albret and Pico dash down the road then turn back. Full of boisterous laughter, they headed toward Terni. There they stopped at a tavern that stayed open all night for Carnaval revelers.

Inside they ordered drinks all around.

"I would say we scared the ladies plenty," said Piero. "Thus we accomplished our main objective. Keep them in fear."

"I wanted to get my hands on some of their jewelry, though," said Ugo.

"I would have relished a sword fight with Albret. I could have won too," boasted Tristano. "The driver would need to manage the horses. So he would have been no problem."

"I told you they had armed guards inside," said Anslo. "Besides, that upstart kid is quite agile with a sword, if I do say so myself."

"I only wanted to snatch the girl's mask for a souvenir," said Niccolini.

"Hush, Niccolini," the three brothers said together.

"You know nothing about banditry," said Piero and ordered more drinks for all.

fourteen

Once inside the walls of their own castle, Costanza and Anabella felt safe and protected. Never in the hundreds of years that Bilivertis had lived here had bandits or enemies of any sort penetrated these walls. Certainly the ladies had been frightened, especially in light of the recent kidnapping, but the chase was easily attributed to wandering bandits. One could expect such encounters during the Carnaval celebrations.

For that matter, memories of the delightful evening easily overshadowed any fear. For Anabella, the gala served as her debut as an eligible young lady. For Costanza, it was her acceptance back into society after the death of her husband. Each claimed significant success.

❧

Costanza paced the walkways of the inner courtyard, contemplating the crops that should be planted. They had large areas of level land conducive to wheat growing, but how could she know the most fertile soil? Where did one buy mulberry trees, and how many years would it take for them to support silkworms? She would need to find an expert to help with this complex industry.

She looked up, startled to see a guard standing in the path. "Pardon me, Signora. A gentleman, a Signore Turati, is at the gate. Do you wish to see him?"

"Yes. Yes, you may escort him to the courtyard. I will receive him here," she said.

As soon as the guard disappeared, she smoothed her eyebrows, fluffed the curls that framed her face, and patted the coif that covered the bun at the crown of her head. She had anticipated this day ever since she had watched his train disappear around the hillside. But today she wore a plain brown dress with little decoration save the lace underskirt and the embroidered panel that framed the open neck. Would he be pleased with her appearance?

Antonio stepped through the doorway in his usual stylish attire and doffed a handsome fur hat with turkey feather, which he placed on a stone bench. He held out both hands to receive hers. His eyes sparkled. For the first time she noticed straight white teeth that showed through his broad smile.

"Costanza! What a joy to see you!" He squeezed her hands and looked into her eyes. "I have longed for this moment since last we stood together. I trust all is well with you. And Anabella; has she recovered?"

"It is good to see you likewise, Antonio. Yes, Anabella has recovered completely," she said with a smile, not wanting to share the anxiety she had endured during her daughter's illness.

"Unfortunately, I can stay only two hours or so. My merchandising train has gone on ahead of me on the way to Rome. I have only my horse. You see, I took a side trip to ask if perhaps you needed some specific goods."

No caffelatte in my kitchen, no songs with his lute? thought Costanza. *He wants to sell me goods? Well, I can be just as businesslike as he.* She let go of his hands. "Yes, Signore Turati, I plan to plant wheat this spring. I will need a quantity of seeds."

"Is that a fact?" said Antonio. He invited her, with a motion from his hand, to sit down on the stone bench. She did so. Taking his fur hat and placing it on his lap, he seated himself beside her.

"And how many bags of wheat do you wish to order, Signora Biliverti?" He took from a pouch a pad of paper, a quill, and ink and sat ready to make a notation.

Costanza twisted her handkerchief in her hands. "You have surprised me with your visit, Signore. I need to consult with my son for the exact amount. And how to plant it. And where."

She looked down at her hands, feeling totally defeated both in business dealings and in possible love.

An awkward silence followed. Antonio shifted his feet, stood, and put on his hat. "Costanza, have a groomsman saddle you a horse. We will ride out and find the best place to plant wheat." He held out his hand to assist her.

She remained seated and did not look up. "That will not be necessary, Signore Turati."

He grabbed her hand and gently pulled her to her feet. "Costanza, my name is Antonio. An–ton–i–o! You do ride, do you not?" The barone would not be rebuffed by her sudden formality.

"Yes, of course, I ride, An–ton–i–o," she said, yielding to his pull. She looked up at him, and all her coolness melted. The fact that she had not been on the back of a horse in three years made no difference now. She could not understand this man's thinking, but neither could she resist him.

&

The two rode first toward the devastated vineyards. While the groomsman had readied her horse, Costanza took time to put on her new leather boots, a fine gray woolen cape, and, unfortunately, a rather frumpy riding hat. She had tried to don Anabella's, but, alas, it was too small.

Antonio had a good view of both boots as she sat side-saddle. "You flatter the boots, dear Costanza. If I had known how very handsome you would make them appear, I would have charged you more."

"You can make it up on the wheat," she said and smiled. She felt free and comfortable with him now as their horses cantered along side by side. "I am intrigued by your hat, Antonio. I have never seen such lustrous fur. What is it, if I may ask?"

"Ah, an advantage of the merchant trade is the opportunity to see new commodities first. The beaver pelt, and the feather as well, came on a ship from the New World. I had it made up for me at a little millinery shop in Genoa. Someday I would love to sail across the ocean and see this vast new land I hear about from the returning sea merchants."

She noticed him staring at her own outmoded bonnet.

"I see you find my *cappello* monstrous, Antonio."

He grinned sheepishly in acknowledgment.

"Then let us be rid of it." She laughed and reached up, unpinned the hat, and flung it into the air. As her hair fell unraveled about her shoulders, she urged her horse to gallop off at full speed.

At the border of an old vineyard, she drew her horse to a halt, tied her unloosed locks back with a ribbon, and dismounted. Antonio had stabbed the disgraceful cappello as it fell to the ground and now raced toward her with his trophy raised high on the tip of his sword. They hitched their horses to saplings and walked over to the dead stubs of grapevines.

"Since I have pierced your poor cappello, may I keep it, Costanza, to remember you always?"

"What poor taste you have!" she said mockingly. "But, as I will never wear it again, I give it to you."

Much to her surprise, he stuffed it inside his doublet.

"So these are the ruined vineyards?"

"Yes. I am thinking of planting mulberry bushes here and eventually starting a silk fabrication. Do you think that would be profitable?"

Unlike his nature he hesitated to give advice.

"As a merchant you travel about and know what is profitable and what is not. I truly value your opinion," she said in an effort to gain knowledge.

"In that case, Costanza, I believe it would be more profitable to raise sheep for the purpose of selling wool. Sheep prefer hills; they do not mind the rocks; they crop the grass. You already have men who shear sheep, do you not? You can easily sell it to the industry in Florence. Very little can go wrong. Sheep, for the most part, are hearty animals. Mulberry bushes are hearty also, but the silkworms must eat the leaves fresh every day. You would need to set up the processing here, which requires many complicated steps."

"But I have noticed that silk is worn more and more. Would not that be an forthcoming business—if I were ready for an increasing market?" She sought facts that would aid her decisions.

"It is true that silk is becoming more popular. But France has already captured the market. They have more favorable trade laws, and my clients are demanding silk from Lyon." He spoke to her as he would any man seeking the same information.

"The investment and risk both would be greater with silk, you think?"

"Yes, that is my opinion. The choice of wheat, however, is an excellent crop for the plains if your soil is rich."

They rode off toward the west to check potential fields on both sides of the river Nera. Antonio, though somewhat amused, took her questions seriously. *But can such an astute, calculating woman be at the same time loving, affectionate, and thoughtful of my needs? I liked the way she threw off that ridiculous hat and galloped away, however. She is, indeed, a mysterious woman,* he thought as he rode along beside her.

❧

The two, still on horseback, concluded their brief visit at the front gate.

"I will deliver the wheat two weeks from today. I think you have chosen the best fertile ground, where the cattle used to graze. Your workers should begin plowing immediately in the manner I suggested."

"And if Marco should reject my idea?"

"Then you are not obligated to purchase the wheat," he said, making a gesture more generous than his usual style.

He dismounted and took hold of her hand to assist her descent. A groomsman led her horse away. Antonio placed his hands gently on her shoulders. "Costanza, when I return with your order, Paolo will be with me. We would like to stay the night."

"Yes, of course." This was not at all an unusual arrangement. Such an isolated client would expect to provide board and lodging.

"And, Costanza, I want us to spend a whole day together. Perhaps we could go to the Cascata della Marmore. Have you been to the cascades recently?"

"Not in many years. I would like that very much, Antonio. I need to get away from the castle, away from all the decisions I have to make."

"But you seem to enjoy calculating and making decisions."

"Sometimes." But she seemed to enjoy them less in his company.

Antonio let his hands slide softly down her arms and to her waist. Then he pulled her close. She yielded to his embrace and relaxed in his arms. He kissed her forehead, and she laid her cheek against his chest.

"May God keep you safe until we are together again." He mounted his horse and rode off in a cloud of dust.

He must ride swiftly since he stayed much past the two hours he allotted. An uneasiness came over her. *Did I impose on his time by asking him all those questions? Men generally do not respect women who discuss masculine subjects. Yet he seemed willing to linger. And he wants to spend a whole day with me. I hope he throws away my hat!*

≈

Just inside the door Anabella stood with hands on hips, like a parent awaiting a naughty child. "Mother! Who was that man, and why did he have his arms around you?"

"Do not be upset, Anabella. That is Antonio Turati. You remember—he is the barone who rescued you."

"He is? I do not recognize him at all," she said in a less agitated voice. "But why is he here now, and why did he embrace you? I watched from the staircase window. How can you let any man but Father put his hands on you?" She turned and ran up the stairs.

Costanza found her daughter in her room, sobbing into her pillow. She sat down beside her and patted her shoulder. Anabella pulled away but let her sobs taper off to a sniffle.

"Anabella, you know I loved your father with all my heart. Never did he have cause to doubt my faithfulness."

"Until now." The girl sniffed.

"No, Anabella, the Scriptures release a widow to remarry. Besides, just because Antonio has shown interest in me—and I enjoy his company—does not mean we are going to marry."

"Then you are not going to see him again. Is that right, Mother?" Anabella sat up, her eyes red, and blew her nose on her handkerchief.

"I have ordered some wheat that we can plant as a new profitable crop. He will deliver it in a fortnight."

"Without consulting Marco?"

"Anabella, your brother is a good son who makes a great effort to perform his duty. He is able to run this seigniory and plans to do so when he arrives this spring. But he is more talented in scientific studies. Originally, your father set aside money for his university education. Jacopo, as you know, was to take over the estate. But he left home at seventeen and never showed any interest in the family business. You know the rest." Costanza took Anabella's hand. "Please understand that this responsibility is new and difficult for Marco."

"Mother, it is newer and even more difficult for you!"

"But my prime is past. I can afford to make sacrifices. He has a young wife to please. Soon they will start a family, I hope. And I want them to fulfill their heart's desire as much as possible."

"And your heart's desire is—is to be with that man? What about me? Does it not concern you that it pains me to see you like that?"

"Yes, Anabella, I care very much."

fifteen

Weighty matters consumed Costanza's time as she strolled in the inner courtyard. She had sent Albret to the homes of the workers she had dismissed earlier in hopes of rehiring them. The ones Marco had let go in the fall were listed in the ledger, but neither she nor Albret knew of their whereabouts. Workers had easily plowed the areas for vegetable gardens. But the new wheat fields took much more time and required replowing and raking, as that ground had never before been cultivated. She herself rode out to observe the work, ensuring that all was done as Antonio had specified.

She worried constantly about Anabella. Although Anabella was polite and sweet spirited around her, Costanza felt pained by her daughter's attitude toward Antonio. *I can give him up,* she thought. *After all, there seemed to be some tension between us on his last visit. Sometimes I do not know what he means, and sometimes I think he puzzles over me. And always I wonder how many women he treats with the same gallantry. Knowing him has been a thrilling experience, but I could be painfully hurt by allowing myself to care about him.*

"Mother." Anabella appeared in the courtyard and interrupted her thoughts. "Mother, may I speak a word with you?" Her tone was gentle and held no animosity.

"Of course, Anabella, but if it is about Antonio, I have already decided. . ."

"No, Mother, it is not really about him. That is your affair, and I have no right to challenge what you do. I have been praying often in the chapel."

"Yes, I have noticed that. Often you go beyond your elders in your steadfast faith."

"It helps me think more clearly, Mother." Then in a more somber tone she said, "I did not tell you about one of the men who kidnapped me."

"But you said they did not. . ."

"I spoke the truth, believe me." She struggled with the confession. "But this one man put his hands where I did not wish. I was helpless to stop him. He was about the same age as the barone, an older man. I think maybe I confused them in my mind. Without knowing why, it upset me terribly."

Costanza put her arms around her daughter and held her close. "My poor, dear Anabella. I am so sorry you had to endure that." Tears welled up in the mother's eyes.

"It still seems strange to think of you with anyone but Father."

"I know."

"Antonio did save my life. I guess I could be a little more charitable," she said with a smile of resignation. Both considered the question of her attitude toward Antonio settled. Anabella returned to her usual vivacious and talkative self. And Costanza, though grieved over learning of her daughter's horrible experience, carried one less worry on her shoulders.

❦

That evening Anabella sought out Albret in the little alcove by the kitchens where he often read by candlelight. They had not had an opportunity to talk since the festivities at the Bargerinos.

"How did you enjoy the Carnaval party the other night, Albret?" she asked, startling him by her presence.

"Oh, it is you, Anabella. Please sit down." His voice was welcoming and gentle.

She took the stool near the window seat and adjusted her skirts. "I wished for you to dance with me, but you seemed to prefer someone else."

"Anabella, you know perfectly well that I danced with no one that night. I have never been trained in the social graces."

His embarrassment at this admission touched her. "You certainly have the bearing of a gentleman."

"Thank you," he said modestly. "But, you, Anabella, you were—well, all the young men found you very attractive."

"I did have a most delightful time. I hope Mother will open the ballroom again and provide some entertainment. She and Father used to offer a social affair at least once a month. Do you have a key to our ballroom?"

"Yes, but I am not sure. . ."

"We will ask Mother tomorrow. If you like, I will show you the dances. Would you like that, Albret?"

"Indeed I would." After a lengthy pause, which Anabella suspected concealed a blush in the darkness, he said, "I learned some news that Pico heard at the Bargerinos. It confirms what we have suspected."

"Please tell me," she said eagerly. She especially enjoyed their partnership in solving mysteries.

"This will be difficult for you, but Anslo is responsible for Sandro's death," he confided.

"So Anslo is the one? Why would he do such a horrible thing?" Repulsed as she was by Anslo, she had never thought of him as a murderer.

"It seems Sandro suspected arson the very night of the fires, as did I. One of our dismissed workers, who now is employed by the Bargerinos, heard Anslo threaten Sandro."

"That does not prove he killed him."

"No, but the worker heard a thud in the bushes, and Anslo returned alone. You should never have been out there, Anabella. He said you returned from the river at about the same time."

"I know I was very foolish. Should we not report this to the authorities?"

"Yes, but first we need to get the worker to agree to testify before the tribunal. There is a greater picture here. What is his connection to the Scullis? We do not want to encourage their wrath at this time."

"You'll dismiss Anslo, will you not? He could be dangerous."

"Yes. I will do it tomorrow. I will need the approval of your mother or of Marco. When will he be here? Do you know?"

"Any day now, Mother says. But perhaps you should tell Mother all you know. She really is a very strong woman."

"Yes, I see her riding around the estate, not missing any activity. She directed the men in clearing the land and cultivating it for wheat. For that I was glad, as I have never done that myself, having grown up in Rome."

"Remember—dance lesson tomorrow in the ballroom, Albret." She rose and took her night candle. "Good night, Albret."

"Good night, Anabella."

Albret watched her drift off into the darkness and disappear up the staircase. *If only I were of noble birth, I could hope to think of her as my bride someday. But, alas, this land and castle go to Marco and his descendants. He married a banker's daughter, but that is much different when it is the man who holds the noble title. No, Marco will want her betrothed to someone like Frederigo Bargerino, with whom she danced so happily the other night.*

&

The next morning Costanza and her attendant, Clarice, sipped caffelatte on the balcony that overlooked the front gate. Although Clarice had been at the castle longer than Costanza and had served her personally for several years, the two women had never been confidants.

When Lorenzino was alive, he and Costanza often found occasions to socialize with others of their status around Terni. At least twice a year they visited his relatives in Rome. The men and women would usually share a meal, perhaps dance, but always end with ample time to talk with those of one's own sex. She especially missed that now. Women did not travel around to seek each other's company without their husbands.

The more masculine pursuits of accounting and directing

the business decisions of the seigniory, she accomplished with skill. But they were lonely endeavors. More lonely still was the constant longing to have her emptiness filled. Thus she had invited Clarice to help her think through some matters.

"Clarice, do you remember when thirty Bilivertis were living in this castle? The women sat around together doing their needlework and watching the little ones. What problems there were, we solved together. Lorenzino and his brothers came to dinner every evening. We even had a priest who held services in our chapel once a month and on special days. The servants worshipped with us. It is a lonely, empty castle now." She turned to her servant for confirmation.

"There was a lot more work then," said Clarice, not sharing her feelings.

Costanza continued with her own view of circumstances. "It seems someone is always leaving. Or arriving, then leaving."

"You mean Marco and his wife?" the other woman said, trying to follow the logic of this conversation.

"Well, yes, Marco. I never know exactly when he will return. When he is here, he is in charge. When he leaves, I am. But not really. I do not know what he will make of my decisions."

"You know, Signora, I cannot comment on matters such as that."

"And then there is the barone, Antonio Turati," she said with some hesitation.

"Yes, of course, that very handsome, charming man. The entire domestic staff took note of him," Clarice said, showing much more interest in Costanza's concerns. She poured them each a second cup of coffee and settled in to listen.

"As you are my loyal attendant, I trust you not to share anything I might say among the other domestics."

"Yes, of course; I have been loyal to this family for many years," said Clarice, somewhat annoyed by the gentle reminder.

"I admit to you, Clarice, that I enjoy the company of Antonio Turati."

"Is that a problem, Signora?"

"The problem is that he leaves. I am left longing every day for his return. I often come out here to this balcony in hopes of seeing him come around that curve in the road, from behind the hill." She looked to see if Clarice thought she was sounding foolish. Noting no change of expression, she continued, "Do you think it is better to have no one in your life to long for? Or is such pain worth the short-lived pleasure?"

"You are asking me a question I have never thought about, Signora. I married Pico when I was fourteen. We have worked here all our married lives. He is a fine man, but I know nothing of passionate love, of that longing you talk about. I think that is something only for the upper classes." She looked at her mistress apologetically, having failed to help her with what seemed to her a frivolous concern.

"Have you never missed anyone, Clarice?"

The woman frowned and searched far back in her memory. This was a woman who lived each day as it came and accepted, without question, the bad with the good. After a few moments, however, she did draw forth a scene from her past. "Yes, Signora, I do miss my mother and my little sister from time to time. But I try not to think of it."

"Do you never see them?" Costanza was suddenly struck by the huge difference between the classes of society. Her servant's life consisted of six long days of work for others with very little personal time. On a rare day off, Clarice might catch a ride with anyone going into Terni. There she might spend the day making small personal purchases. On Sundays Pico had access to a carriage and would take some of the servants to church with them. There, classes mixed freely. But they had never taken several days to visit relatives. She had never before thought of her having relatives.

"Where does your family live, Clarice?"

"I don't know, Signora. All I remember is that Pico's parents came to my house one day. We were very poor, and I had no dowry. They gave my father some money and told me I belonged to them now. My sister cried and clung to my skirts as they took me from the house. I did not even look back to see my mother one last time. In a way I was glad. My father was a very brutal man." The servant stopped abruptly.

"I did not know your story. And I should have known. You have served me faithfully for many years," Costanza said, full of remorse for having taken this woman for granted. "You and Pico never had children?"

"No. He was angry about that at first. I was disappointed also, but I think it has saved me a lot of pain. You miss Marco when he is gone. And I know the anguish you endured over Anabella. And then this Turati fellow. No, to answer your question, if you want my opinion, I think it is better not to have people in your life that you are always missing or longing for or upset about. But that is just my opinion. Who am I to say?"

"Clarice, I value what you have to say. Thank you very much. I will remember your words." Costanza gave the woman's hand a squeeze, so touched was she by her story.

Clarice took the coffee tray and returned to her chores. Costanza took up her needlework and pondered the servant's opinion. She looked down the road to the bend around the hill. Antonio should arrive today or tomorrow—or the next day. *Before this painful longing turns to love, perhaps I should tell An–ton–i–o not to come back again.*

sixteen

Albret turned the key in the lock of the large wooden door. Anabella stood excitedly at his side. The door creaked open to musty smells. Both stepped inside the huge ballroom and looked around, from ceiling to stained-glass windows. Carved Renaissance-style chairs and benches, covered with dust, lined the walls. A shallow dome in the ceiling held a magnificent array of boy angels flitting through blue sky. Various men and women in fluttering robes also sailed upward.

"Is that a biblical picture?" asked Albret, awestruck.

"I am not sure what it is. When I was a child it always fascinated me, but I never asked about it," said Anabella. Having not been in the room for three years, she saw everything in a new light, but she was also engulfed by happy memories of festivities from the past. Two of the inner walls were covered in huge tapestries, mostly of historic or hunting scenes. One, however, was of a near-nude couple adoring each other among flowers and fruit trees. It had never embarrassed Anabella before, but now she decided to divert Albret's attention to the oil paintings. "This one," she pointed out, "is Abraham starting to sacrifice Isaac."

"And here is the ram, caught by his horns, who will be the real sacrifice," said Albret. "Could this be by Tintoretto? It is certainly in his style."

"I do not know. You will have to ask Bianca about that. She knows all about the artists."

"This is a more magnificent room than the Bargerinos have," observed Albret, not wishing to pursue a subject not interesting to Anabella.

Their steps echoed as they walked toward the center of the

room. "Now, for the dance lesson I promised you," said Anabella, feeling shy to be alone with Albret in this grand ballroom.

He put his hand lightly on her waist and took her hand. "Now what?" he said, feeling even more shy than his partner. Anabella rose to the occasion and began her instruction. Albret easily caught on to the steps, and soon they gained a semblance of what one might call a dance. They laughed at their mistakes. It was great fun, especially as they began to feel more at ease.

"If we only had a little music," complained Albret.

"Is that why you keep stepping on my toes?" she said, giggling. "Mother said she would be here shortly, but she must have forgotten."

Suspecting they might remain unsupervised, Albret attempted some of the fancy steps he had observed at the ball, then twirled her around.

At that moment, they both became aware of music that fit their maneuvers exactly. They froze in midswing and stared toward the music.

On a brocaded Renaissance chair next to the door sat Antonio Turati, playing his lute. "Continue—continue, my dears. I am here to enhance the dance, not halt it!"

Anabella felt uncomfortable in the barone's presence, but Albret, having no clue about her feelings, started up the steps again. Indeed he proudly showed off all he had learned. Anabella gave in to his lead, and together they danced to the end of Antonio's tune.

He clapped enthusiastically as the young couple approached him. "What a pleasure to see you, Anabella, and in such good health. I hardly recognize you. And, Albret, what a fine escort you make."

"Good afternoon, Signore Turati," said Anabella as graciously as possible. "I will inform Mother that you are here." She started to walk past him in an effort to escape under the pretense of finding her mother.

"No need, my dear. I have been announced. Surely you do not think I would barge into this castle without proper procedures."

"Nor could you, Signore Turati," added Albret. "We are guarded here around the clock as I am sure you have noticed." He graciously shook the older man's hand in a gesture of welcome.

After a few more pleasantries, Costanza arrived. Anabella excused herself. Albret noticed a special joy between this merchant and the signora and wondered if perhaps more was here than amicable business dealings. The three of them walked out to Antonio's carriage where Paolo waited with the wheat Costanza had ordered. Antonio gave her a good price, which she accepted without bargaining. Antonio explained to both Costanza and Albret how the wheat should be planted and suggested they have the workers begin tomorrow. Albret asked several questions to make certain all would be done properly.

"I feel this process is in good hands, Albret," said Antonio. "You will be the one to direct it all. You see, Costanza and I will not be around tomorrow."

"Do you not think we should be, Antonio? I have observed every step of the plowing and raking," said Costanza. This had become her project. Even though she had great faith in Albret, she hesitated to leave at the critical planting time.

Antonio took off his hat and scratched his head. "Albret, why don't you assemble the workers at daybreak? Give your instructions and start the planting. Costanza and I will come by the fields and see how it is going. We can stay until you, Costanza, and I, as the so-called expert, agree that all is as it should be. What do you say?"

"Yes, that would be satisfactory, Antonio," said Costanza.

Antonio suggested they all ride out in the carriage now to see if the fields were properly prepared. They would have enough time for the little excursion before nightfall and the dinner which the servants were already preparing for the guests.

ॐ

The little group stood at the edge of the fields, admiring how finely it had been tilled. *This man always stands ready with practical solutions,* Costanza thought. *Perhaps I should not let him go so easily.*

While commenting on the perfect location and the potential profit of such an investment, they heard the pounding of horse hooves behind them. They turned to see Marco dismount and walk briskly toward them.

"Hello, Mother," he said, obviously upset. "And which of you two is Signore Turati?" He looked back and forth between Antonio and Paolo.

"That would be. . . ," Antonio began.

"Marco, there must be a misunderstanding," interrupted Costanza. "Why would you be upset toward. . . ?"

"Signore Turati, I am Marco Biliverti, marchese of this estate. I am the one who makes the decisions of what to plant and when. Can you explain yourself as to why you are here taking advantage of my widowed mother by inducing her to buy and plant your wheat? And for what reason you. . . ?"

"Yes, Marchese Biliverti, I would be pleased to explain myself," said Antonio, extending his hand. "But first please allow your mother to explain how we came to meet. Then I will clarify to your satisfaction, I hope, why she made the decision to plant wheat and why she ordered the seed from me."

Marco was trembling with anger, but he was still a gentleman. He shook Antonio's hand firmly. "All right, Mother, under what conditions did you meet this—this person?"

"Marco, I have longed for your return. It saddens me to see you so angry and without cause." She looked imploringly up at her son whom she loved and so admired.

"Mother, it is not you for whom I hold anger. I want to protect you as Father always did. That is my duty. I should never have gone back to Padua." He embraced her lovingly. Albret, as well as Paolo and Antonio, stood stunned, not knowing to what to attribute his outburst.

"Much has happened, Marco, in your absence. I will tell you the details when we return to the castle. I cannot imagine why you are distressed. Antonio is my friend. We owe him a debt of gratitude. You see, your sweet sister, Anabella, was kidnapped for ransom."

"But I just talked with her at the castle. She is the one who told me I could find that man here at the fields—that you are going to plant wheat you bought from him." He sputtered out the words dumbfounded.

"Marco, it has been several weeks since that tragedy. Antonio Turati saved her life from her captors and brought her back to me." Marco, now subdued, turned pale with shock. "To plant wheat was my decision. Since I knew Antonio as an honest merchant, I chose to buy from him and to seek his advice."

Costanza was relieved to see Marco somewhat abashed at his own quick judgment. He now turned to the older man. "Forgive me, Signore Turati. I have been a fool. How can you ever forgive me?"

Marco, sincere in his contrition, remained confused by his mother's decisions, the kidnapping, and the usurpation of his position, if not by the barone, then by his mother.

&

What should have been a happy reunion was permeated with conflict, misunderstandings, and guilt. The next morning the group sat around the familial table after breakfast, each trying desperately to ease tensions and explain their own sincere motives. After hearing the details, Marco was overcome with grief over his sister's kidnapping and consumed with guilt for having left his family vulnerable for a second time. But he wanted all to know that he took his duty to his mother and sister very seriously. Bianca surmised that she had swayed her husband to tarry too long in Padua. But he reveled so in working with the esteemed scientist, and she found those in the university community much more accepting of her as a female artist. Should she turn her back on opportunities?

Anabella bore a portion of guilt herself for misleading Marco about Antonio's presence. What she had spoken was true, but she had left out so much of the picture that Marco easily filled in false assumptions. If her tone was negative, she was sorry, for truly she felt much gratitude toward the barone.

Costanza, who had relished her project of the wheat fields, now recognized that she had overstretched her role and usurped the male authority of her son. She knew the rules and had lived comfortably by them all her life—until now. At this point, she confessed to having arranged to purchase several ewes to increase their flock of sheep—for the purpose of entering the wool industry.

Marco, astounded at her boldness, announced that he had already arranged for the vineyards to be replanted with quick-growing vines. It would take several years, but he felt certain that in his lifetime, through grafting, he could again attain the quality of wine for which the Bilivertis were famous. Costanza deferred to Marco and agreed to cancel her order of ewes.

Albret was absent, having arisen early to organize the workers for planting the wheat. Antonio sat silently, observing these family squabbles. He had meant only to be helpful to this widow who had sought his advice. And yet he held a greater, more personal, interest. But perhaps it would be better for all if he removed himself from the situation. He offered up a silent prayer for this distraught family and left it in the hands of God. Paolo rolled his eyes at Antonio and remained silent also.

Antonio had made a commitment to Costanza to spend this day with her. Being an honorable man he would honor that. When a pause fell in the discussion, he seized the moment and stood. "Costanza, since we are riding to the Cascata della Marmore today, we should be on our way. If all of you will excuse us—?" He bowed courteously.

seventeen

Before breakfast Costanza had dressed for riding—except for a decent cappello. She had had so much to think about that she had forgotten to remake something appropriate for today's ride. Perhaps she could fashion one quickly from an old hat of Lorenzino's.

At the moment she opened her mouth to excuse herself at the bottom of the staircase, Antonio said, "Costanza, I have brought you something." He handed her an object wrapped in a silken cloth. "I hope you find it to your taste."

She unwrapped the cloth to discover a most elegant beaver riding hat. "It is beautiful, Antonio. You needn't have!"

"It is merely a replacement. You remember I pierced a hole in your other one." They both laughed in recalling the hat incident. The laughter lifted the strain of the breakfast discussion. "Go on upstairs," he said. "I know you will want a mirror to try it on. But I assure you it will fit. I had it made for you by the measure of the other."

"It is most stylish, Antonio. Exactly what I would have chosen for myself. Thank you," she said with a smile and ascended the stairs.

ᴥ

Finally the two were ready and mounted on their horses. Costanza had packed a lunch and tied the basket to her saddle. The hat proved to be very becoming, adding height to her figure. The smooth beaver pelt sported tips of three turkey feathers.

But before leaving she expressed concern over riding out alone, just the two of them. She suggested that at least two guards accompany them. "We were nearly ambushed by bandits the other night," she told him. "And Anabella's kidnappers

115

could still be lurking about. Do you not think it would be prudent?"

"If you would feel more secure with guards, I can accept that," said Antonio with a hint of disappointment in his voice. "I want you to be comfortable. I am skilled with my sword, here at my waist. And I carry a flintlock pistol and powder under my cloak. It is my habit to stay armed, as I usually have merchandise to protect. For that matter, Costanza, bandits most often strike at night. We are carrying nothing valuable."

"Except my cappello." She grinned.

"I think I can defend that. Do you wish to enlist the guards?"

Costanza frowned. It would be wonderful to escape the castle with its stressful atmosphere—and be alone, just the two of them. "I agree—we do not need to enlist guards," she said. "I do feel secure in your company. Let us be on our way."

March weather in the Italian countryside framed a spectacular background for these two. Sunlight streamed behind them over the summit of rocky cliffs, tall cypress trees cast sword-thin shadows, songbirds chirped their mating songs, and early spring wildflowers bloomed along their path. It was, indeed, a splendid morning for riding.

Both were delighted to find Albret skillfully supervising the planting. Paolo had arrived just ahead of them to help. The workers had already covered much of the plowed earth. Assured that all was well, they stayed only briefly. After a few words of praise and encouragement, they galloped off to the west toward the town.

In Terni they rode past a fascinating mixture of ancient Roman architecture, Renaissance, and the more modern Baroque. "Do you know where to find the ruins?" asked Antonio.

"We need to follow the Via Roma to the outskirts of town," said Costanza as they turned onto the old road constructed of marble slabs. Once at the ruins, they dismounted to survey the toppled capitals, the horizontal columns, and fragments of ancient statues.

"A magnificent temple to Jupiter once stood here. But, of course, you have seen far grander ruins in Rome," said Costanza, seating herself on a capital with carvings of acanthus leaves.

"Yes, but I am still amazed at what the ancient civilizations were able to accomplish. Look at the face of this woman, carved so perfectly, with her curls neatly in place about her forehead," said Antonio, running his hands over the severed head of a statue.

"Poor young thing; she has lost her nose," said Costanza lightheartedly. "What ruins do you suppose our generation will leave for people to find a thousand years from now?"

"Do you suppose the Basilica of St. Peter, now being enlarged, will still be standing? Probably not. Michelangelo's painting of creation in the Sistine Chapel is already a hundred years old. But could it survive another nine hundred years?"

"Or think about all his wonderful statues of Moses, of David, and the others he created. Do you imagine someone will someday pick up David's head and declare it perfect. . . ?"

"Except for a broken nose," said Antonio. "Those would all be objects of our Christian faith, as this probably is the head of a Roman goddess. Their religion has passed away."

"But I believe Christianity is eternal," said Costanza firmly. "What do you think, Antonio?"

"Yes, I told you I believe our God exists," said Antonio. "I have given much thought to what you said before—that He really cares about us. I have tried to pray more and believe in Him more. At the table this morning while all in your family were talking at once and trying to explain themselves, I prayed silently that you would understand each other. I have always found disagreements unpleasant, and understanding is very important to me. A calm peace came over me. Did you not say something about God giving a kind of peace that surpasses understanding?"

"Yes, Antonio, I know the exact Scripture verse. It is found in Paul's epistle to the Philippians: 'In every thing by prayer and supplication with thanksgiving let your requests be made known unto God. And the peace of God, which passeth understanding, shall keep your hearts and minds through Christ Jesus.'"

"So you think God did hear my prayer? Perhaps He gave me peace even when I did not understand," said Antonio, a questioning look on his face.

"I see your faith growing, Antonio. God does care about you and what happens in our lives." Costanza found herself delighted that Antonio was discovering these truths. "And as to my family understanding each other, they will eventually. We love one another very much and respect each other's feelings. Because of Marco's love for Bianca, he has decided that women should be on an equal footing with men in all aspects of life. But I believe he still has trouble granting the same to his mother."

"I struggle with some of these ideas myself," admitted Antonio. "But I like very much what I see in this woman sitting before me. Shall we go search for those cascades?" He took her hand to help her up but continued to clasp it as they walked toward their grazing horses.

❧

The horses trotted along briskly for an hour or so. "Are you sure this is the right path, Antonio?" asked Costanza. In her memory the falls were not so far from the town.

"I believe so. But, like you, I have not been here in years. When my merchandising train was returning from Rome, sometimes I would leave it in charge of others and come here alone to think and enjoy the beauty. Look ahead. I believe they lie just beyond those high hills, somewhere in that thick wooded area."

They picked up their pace, and soon Antonio indicated by holding out his arm that they should halt. "Listen!" The roar of the falls in the distance summoned them.

"It is like music!" whispered Costanza.

They rode with renewed anticipation into the wooded hills. The terrain became increasingly rocky and steep. They tied their horses and continued toward the roar on foot. As they reached the top of the precipice, the roar exploded into thunderous rumblings. Antonio took Costanza's hand and pulled her up to where she could see. They stood side by side transfixed. The rushing waters fell from 541 feet, cascading over three huge successive drops down sheer walls of marble. At the bottom, the water swirled into a ravine and disappeared behind the budding trees. Built by the ancient Romans to prevent flooding in the plains, the Cascata della Marmore remained the highest waterfall in Europe.

As they stood there drinking in the beauty, hand in hand, Costanza thought happiness could never surpass this moment. Antonio turned toward her, removed his hat, and swept her into his arms. In an instant she felt his warm, moist lips pressing against hers. She closed her eyes and yielded to his fond embrace. Inside she felt like a young girl of sixteen, experiencing for the first time the overflowing emotion of romance. *I believed these feelings would never stir again,* she thought. *But the thrill is the same at whatever age.*

Antonio said something, but she could not hear over the deafening sound. He clasped her hand and indicated they make a descent. The roaring faded behind the cliff. "We left your lunch basket tied to the saddle. The height of the sun and my stomach indicate it is time to eat. Shall we?"

They found an open grassy spot, away from the full impact of the sound but in view of the swirling waters. Costanza spread a large cloth on the ground. "The lunch is rather austere, you know," she said, "because of the Lenten season."

Antonio found the cheeses, bread, olives, and candied fruit delicious and quite ample. He leaned back against the trunk of a gnarled tree and drank water from his flask. "I want to tell you of my past, Costanza," he said in a voice of confession.

"Yes, I want to know everything about Antonio Turati, barone of Florence," she said in eager anticipation.

"Well, perhaps I should begin with the barone part. You see, unlike the revered name of Biliverti, my title was purchased from the duke of Tuscany."

He read surprise in her eyes but continued. She should know this shameful truth. "I met all the criteria, of course. I paid a large sum and served the prince honorably. The Tuscan Order of Santo Stefano accepted me as a full member. Throughout the Italian states and across southern France, I am generally hailed as a knowledgeable and fair merchant. I have worked scrupulously to build and maintain an honorable reputation. Legally my title is not fraudulent, but I feel it is inferior nonetheless. I purchased it, of course, to raise my status, but I know in reality that I rank far below the deposed nobles who beg on the streets of Rome. At least, noble blood still runs in their veins." He tried to read her face. Was rejection or acceptance written there?

"Antonio, I admit I am surprised, even stunned perhaps. I had just assumed. . . But that does not change at all my high regard for you. And I respect you for your honesty," she finally said, choosing her words carefully.

It was not the overwhelming acceptance he had hoped for, but it was enough. "What about your heritage, Costanza?"

"My family lived in a country villa outside Rome. The land was not nearly so vast as the Biliverti estate. We are distant relatives of the Medici family—'poor relatives,' my father used to say. We were not poor, of course, but in comparison to Lorenzo the Magnificent and the rest of his clan, he grieved that we were not nearly so renowned. Always he was proud of his Medici blood, however. I was the youngest of five children. We were taught at home, the girls as well as the boys, by a tutor who changed often. My father was more strict than we would have liked, but for the most part, I have happy memories of those times. Mother was kind but not affectionate. I think that is why I dote on Anabella, to make up for that loss. They are all dead now, except for my brother in Rome. What was your boyhood like?"

"I am glad you have happy memories, Costanza. My childhood was not so pleasant, I am afraid." He hesitated, reluctant to share more truth from his past. But that was precisely why he planned this time alone with her. He knew he cared deeply for her, and if rejection were inevitable, sooner would be preferable to later.

"Please tell me. I want to know the little boy Antonio," she said to encourage him.

"To begin with, my family was counted among the poor in Florence. We led a miserable life, although I remember little of it before my mother died in childbirth. I believe I was about six years old. My uncle and aunt took the baby to raise along with their four children. My father had trouble finding odd jobs because he was infirm. Something was wrong with his legs that made it difficult to walk. We would fish in the Arno which was not far from our little hut. Sometimes he would send me to the markets late in the day to gather scraps that were left for the beggars. Being small, I could not fight over food as well as the others."

"My heart breaks for that small boy," said Costanza. She appeared truly touched by his story.

"There is more. My father became bedfast. I tried to take care of him, but I did not know what to do. Finally I walked several miles to my uncle's house. I think he was angry, but he took us in. They too were poor, but at least there were other children. My baby sister had died by then. My aunt always complained of being tired and overworked. I realize now how true that was with all the laundry, cooking, cleaning, and caring for my father—who only yelled at her.

"When Father died, my uncle said he could not keep me anymore. I will never forget that day. He wrapped up some extra clothes and food in a bundle no bigger than this"—he pointed to the picnic basket. "He said that he was sorry, but I was a strong and smart lad. I could make it on my own now. And, as you can see, I did."

Costanza shook her head in unbelief.

"That was the worst part. Well, almost. I was about nine years old but looked older. My cousin had taught me how to get jobs guarding someone's carriage. You had to ask in a very professional way, then grin and look directly in their eyes. I became very good at it. Sometimes I fished. It was summer, and, frankly, I enjoyed the freedom. I slept under a bridge with other urchins. But I knew winter would be hard.

"Along with a couple of my new friends, I found myself a real job in the wool industry. It was the lowest work. We worked very hard from sunup to sundown, carding and combing the wool into slivers. But they gave us two meals a day and an indoor place to sleep.

"On Sundays, our one day off, I would go to the Piazzo del Duomo. I loved the beautiful church. I would scatter the pigeons or watch the people. Sometimes a kind person would give me something, but I had no need to beg. One day a well-dressed man in a carriage stopped and walked directly over to me. 'Young man,' he said. I thought I had done something wrong until he continued. 'Would you be interested in an apprenticeship?' I assured him I most certainly would, not even knowing what kind of apprenticeship.

"He took me to his house, which was the most splendid building I had ever been inside, except a church. He said I was sickly, even though I did not think so. He let me bathe, gave me good clothes without any holes, and fed me more food than I could eat. His wife treated me like her own child. Their children had married and left home. I came to love those two people with all my heart. But I could not understand why they were doing this.

"At first I was frightened and thought they might sell me into slavery or something, but the kindness continued. He said he had several friends who took in apprentices in various trades. I chose wool since I already knew something about it. After about three weeks, I went to live at a farm where I was taught to shear sheep. I did not mind the hard work as I felt strong and happy. I was the youngest, but they treated me with respect. I found out later it was because of the man who had brought me there. The couple came to check on me a few times, and I spent one Christmas at their house. Then we lost contact.

"In the winter we worked at other wool industry jobs. The farmer brought in a tutor who taught us to read and write. That opened a whole new world to me. Books were hard to come by, but I read everything I could. Gradually I moved up in the industry. By the time I was seventeen, merchants sought me out to judge the wool at auction. I began to buy and sell a little. In three years I had saved enough to rent a place of my own in Florence. I still had very little, but I thought myself rich enough to marry, which I did. Margherita was a wonderful woman. But I lost both her and our baby boy." Antonio turned his head away and allowed the tears to stream down his face.

After a few moments he continued. "That about sums up my life. Except I did gradually build up a prosperous merchandising business. After I discovered the library in Florence, I would go there and spend hours reading. They would not let you enter unless you were dressed appropriately. I followed their rules. A book cannot be taken home without the order of the duke himself. It took some time, but I eventually made the duke's acquaintance, and now I can read anything I want at my leisure. For that matter I have a library of my own."

"That is a sad and also beautiful story," said Costanza. "I admire the way you have done so much with so little. You are truly an amazing man."

Costanza shared some about her married life and the sad story of her stepson, Jacopo, who would never accept her. How he had brought shame to the Biliverti name. More details about their exile in Rome. How she had, without intending to, taken charge of the seigniory. About the fires, the cattle theft, dealing with the fraudulent Niccolini Sculli who sought a betrothal with Anabella.

The intimacy of sharing their lives forced each of them to forget an earlier resolve to end the relationship. And as barriers fell, love made a tentative entrance.

"Costanza," said Antonio, leaning over to take her hand. "When we stood on the precipice earlier, I said something to you."

"Yes, but I could not hear you for the thundering falls."

"I know. Thus I must repeat my words," he said as he pulled her close beside him. He circled his arm around her shoulders, and they sat leaning against the trunk of the old tree, facing a glimpse of white water at the bottom of the ravine. "Costanza," he said, "I love you."

eighteen

They crossed through the town of Terni at midafternoon. Costanza was somewhat tired from the travel but exhilarated by the closeness she felt to Antonio. The words "I love you" echoed in her mind. Somehow she had not been able to say them back to him. The fact that he had purchased a title still puzzled her. Among her noble friends, jokes about such status-grabbing people circulated freely. Generally they were not considered of equal rank. But how could she think of Antonio as inferior? Surely she could consider him an exception to the rule.

She needed to be certain about their love. She wanted the wholehearted approval of Marco and Anabella. And she knew reality awaited her back at the castle.

They had passed few other travelers today. But each time they did, they slowed and spoke a friendly word of greeting. They were now on the road that led to the Biliverti castle. Up ahead they spied a group of horsemen trotting along at a brisk pace toward them.

"It is strange that someone would be coming this way," said Costanza. "Perhaps they are friends of Marco who know he is back."

As they came closer she could tell they were finely dressed in capes and riding hats. The dust stirred up by the horses' hooves stung her eyes, and she lifted her handkerchief to cover her face. They slowed as did the horsemen.

"Good afternoon, signores. I trust you are enjoying this fine spring weather," said Antonio, tipping his hat.

"Good afternoon to you, Signore and Signora," said a hurried voice. The horsemen immediately picked up their speed and galloped on.

"Antonio!" said Costanza, much alarmed. "That was the voice, I am sure, of Piero Sculli. Anabella could be in danger. He is the man who came to arrange a betrothal to his brother."

"That should not present a danger. I am sure Marco can manage the situation," said Antonio. "But certainly we shall see for ourselves." They quickened their pace and sped toward the castle.

❧

When they arrived, groomsmen met them and took the horses. Inside Costanza and Antonio found a little group in the reception room as eager to tell what had transpired as they were to hear it. Marco and Bianca, Albret and Anabella, and Paolo sat discussing the event excitedly.

"What happened? Were the Scullis here?" said Costanza. "Anabella, are you all right?"

"Yes, Mother, I am fine. I watched it all from the staircase window. Marco is the one who knows everything, and he has not even finished telling us," said Anabella, more energized by the strange happenings than frightened.

"And Paolo and I rode up from the fields as the Scullis slunk away. They looked defeated," said Albret.

"Well, Marco, we are listening. What is this about?" said Antonio, taking a seat next to Costanza but being careful to keep a discreet distance.

Marco stood to make his presentation. "Mother and Signore Turati, as I have told the others, the Scullis were here to demand *contrappasso,* compensation. . ."

"And for what possible reason?" exclaimed Costanza.

"I am getting to that. It seems that Jacopo owed all four of them. . ."

"There are four Sculli bothers, Mother," interjected Anabella. "The two others, besides Niccolini and Piero, are the ones who kidnapped me. I never saw them that night, but I heard them talking. I could recognize those ugly voices anywhere."

"And Ugo," said Albret. "You said you heard them from the

window address one as Ugo."

"Yes, Ugo was the man who carried me away on his horse."

"How terrible!" said Costanza, shock written across her face. "Did you know, at the time, they were Niccolini's brothers who had captured you?"

"No. But I did hear them mention Niccolini's name. I thought they had been hired by him to force me to marry him. I did not tell you that, Mother, because I did not want to worry you further. And also because for a time those details were blocked mercifully out of my mind. I was home safe, and I have been very careful since."

"Albret and I have something else to tell you before we resume the Sculli tale," said Marco. Albret then related the gossip he had heard at the Bargerinos the night of Carnaval. "When he told me that, I knew I must dismiss Anslo immediately. We will file charges with the authorities as soon as we know all the facts and can get the worker in question to testify."

"Did he show anger at his dismissal, Marco?"

"Well, yes, he was angry and eager to leave. Albret was with me. He suggested we get a confession from him before he left. Anslo does not know for certain that I know he killed Sandro, but I told him I know a lot about his activities and that he was a spy. I said when he went before the tribunal I would have the power to ask for leniency. We got him to admit that he spied for the Scullis. He even told us the Scullis murdered Jacopo, though he claimed he was not at all involved in that; he only heard them talking about it. I told him the guards would have orders to take him down if ever he set foot on this property again."

"And so why did the Scullis demand contrappasso?" asked Antonio.

"Can you believe that?" said Marco. "I would not let them enter our home. I insisted on meeting them at the front gate. They politely got down off their horses and made some very ridiculous claims."

"You said Jacopo owed them money? This is very strange," said Bianca.

"Piero, who did most of the talking, said that they and Jacopo were in the employ of King Philip of Spain. Jacopo was their commander. He received instructions from the king's representatives about certain projects and negotiated their salaries. Jacopo received the money for all of them, but he never distributed it to them. Now they demand contrappasso from me as the next-of-blood kin—since, they claim, Jacopo was randomly killed by bandits."

"But they were his murderers! Did you not just say Anslo told you so?" exclaimed Costanza in disbelief.

"They did not know that I knew—at that point at least. They claim they were further insulted by our family's refusing to merge with theirs in a marriage contract. He said if we make just restitution, they will consider the matter closed. But if I refuse, he will consider it an affront. Then he reminded me that 'an affronted man is a dangerous one.' "

"That is an outright threat," said Costanza. "It sounds like a vendetta."

"I did refuse, Mother. We owe nothing to the Scullis. Rather, the opposite is true, as you shall see. At that point, he handed me an official Document of Challenge, all witnessed and notarized. I found it rather comical for them to be so formal. Then Tristano, one of the brothers, stepped forward and tried to hand me a glove, meaning he was challenging me to a duel. He said he demanded satisfaction for all of them, as they all had been equally wronged. But I would fight against him alone. As the challenged party, I could choose the weapons, he said. I told him I had learned the new courtly manners that required an honorable man to keep his emotions under control, but if they wished to discuss wrongs, I could list wrongs. 'First of all,' I said, 'it was you who murdered my brother. And second of all. . .' " He stopped suddenly and turned to his mother.

"Mother, this is something I learned just before my marriage to Bianca. It broke my heart to tell her, and we have not discussed it since." He turned to his wife. "Please forgive me for mentioning this now, dear Bianca. I know it is painful for you."

Bianca paled but sat up straight and courageously. "Of course, Marco; everyone needs to know this."

"Jacopo confessed this to me before I escaped from his clutches," said Marco. "He did it to hurt me because he knew I loved Bianca. He confessed that it was he, along with his allies, who took her brother Roberto's life in the name of the king of Spain. I am sure he did not know they were related at the time, and I had not even met Bianca then."

"I do know that Roberto had exposed some unseemly business practices," said Bianca. "That made him a target for those who profited from such practices, but our family had always assumed he had simply succumbed to banditry."

Marco resumed the tale. "I said to the Scullis, 'Second of all, you, along with Jacopo, murdered my wife's brother also. You, of course, did not know that at the time. But, now that you do, how can you possibly think I would reimburse you for taking my brother-in-law's life? Your projects were not committed by order of King Philip—who is a very pious, though simple, man. His underlings had their own little schemes going, and you, Brothers Sculli, profited from helping them along. And, third, you are the party who kidnapped my sister. You assumed I would not find that out. What a despicable and dastardly act that was! And you think it was an insult to refuse you a betrothal? You have no honor to uphold, no wrongs to be righted, no restitution to claim! But, on the other hand, the Bilivertis have much to avenge—the lives of our brother, scoundrel that he was, and our honorable brother-in-law. Besides the harm done our dear, pure, and pious sister! Unlike the shameful cowards you are, we are civilized citizens and rely on the courts for our justice. Be gone,' I said, 'and never set foot on our seigniory again!' "

Bianca led the applause. Marco sat down beside her and took her hand. "Thank you all," he said. "I hope this battle is over, and we will never hear from the Scullis again. Signore Turati, I regret your being dragged into our family matters."

"There is no problem," he said, smiling at Costanza. "I stepped into these matters when I picked up Anabella on the roadside. I have no regrets. Your enemies are my enemies."

⁊❧

Antonio left the next morning, full of love and hope. He had found the woman with whom he wished to spend the rest of his life.

The family Biliverti settled down to warm and loving relationships. Marco admitted that his desire to replant the vineyards came more from feelings of nostalgia than from practical, financial considerations. The more he realized how involved his mother had become in the business affairs of the estate, the more decisions he allowed her. He found her notes in the ledgers precise and accurate. Bianca convinced him that even mothers were worthy of equality and should, at times, be trusted to make sound judgments. The ewes for springtime lambing were reordered.

Unlike her mother and sister-in-law, Anabella loved everything pertaining to home life. She enjoyed time in the kitchens, learning the art of pasta making and other skills. She assisted the chef in planning daily menus. She devised extravagant, seven-course dinners that she hoped, one day, could be used for gala affairs at the castle. Her mother and Bianca agreed with her that they should plan to host a celebration of some sort soon.

Now that wildflowers were bursting up everywhere, Anabella enjoyed gathering bouquets for the table. She stayed close by the castle, however, and never went beyond the wall without a guard or, when possible, Albret.

After long neglect, she returned to the pleasures of sewing for her *cassone*. Marco had mentioned a nobleman he had met in Venice who would be suitable for her. Although a widower in his thirties, he had no children. Marco did not know him well, but friends of his vouched for an honorable reputation, a solid family lineage, and the inheritance of a fine palace and lands.

With Marco's blessings, Costanza enjoyed the details of managing the seigniory and working closely with Albret. She wanted to know each employee by name, something of his family, and an assurance of his loyalty. Often she made calculations and decisions that she passed on to Marco, who then saw to their accomplishment.

Marco spent much time in correspondence with those in the scientific world. He studied books, carried out experiments, and made notes on a daily basis. In the evenings he would share his findings with Albret. The two became close friends.

Bianca spent hours at her easel. Often she would ask Anabella to pose for her. Her favorite subjects were biblical narratives. Anabella became Rebekah at the well, Mary in the flight to Egypt, and Jairus's daughter, whom Jesus raised from the dead. Bianca said she painted to the glory of God, which pleased Anabella immensely.

Now that the Scullis had been conquered, the members of the household pursued their interests with joy and in security. Costanza reported often on the growth of the green blades of wheat. Everyone took pleasure in the new lambs that were being born daily.

One day a messenger delivered a letter to Marco. He was surprised and flattered to notice that the seal indicated the grand duke of Tuscany. As the family had finished the evening meal and was still seated around the table, he decided to open it in their presence. But he read the entire letter in silence.

"Marco, are you going to tell us why you have received a letter from the grand duke?" asked Bianca impatiently.

"Yes, but first there is wonderful news about my professor,

Galileo. You remember I was helping him with his experiments. Mostly I took notes on the observations he made and then wrote them out for him. Since he felt rushed to get his book on the stars out, he permitted me to compose some of his thoughts for the writing. Well, *Sidereus Nuncius* was published in Venice not long before I left. Already it is an international success! A Sir Henry Wotton of England predicts that Galileo is destined to become either exceedingly famous or exceedingly ridiculous. Most hail him as a genius, as do I. But, unfortunately, he has his critics, who say that what he sees through his telescope is mere illusion. He has, however, won over the grand duke of Tuscany, who has invited him to live at his court in Florence as the chief mathematician and philosopher.

"In two weeks Galileo will arrive. The duke is hailing him with an elaborate reception at the palace. Artists, writers, scientists, and representatives of the church will be there. Bianca, you and I are invited!"

"Oh, Marco, we will go, will we not?" exclaimed Bianca. "I so want to meet some of the artists I know will be there. Do you mind if we go, Mother Costanza? It will be such a wonderful opportunity for both our pursuits."

"Of course, Dear. You do not need my permission. I am very proud of your artistic accomplishments. And Marco too. What an honor to work with such a famous man! By all means, go, and have a wonderful time."

"Are you sure, Mother? I do want to do what is right and honorable."

"You want to take good care of me as your father did. That is a noble thing to do. But back then my life was full, raising you and Anabella. Nothing could have made me happier. But now I rather enjoy taking care of myself and learning new things."

"But twice before when I left, tragedy of one sort or the other struck. I vowed never to leave you and Anabella vulnerable again," said Marco.

"And those tragedies were brought on by the Sculli brothers, whom you vanquished. You have already performed the duty of an honorable and courageous son. Go, both of you, with my blessing!"

nineteen

Albret took his meals with the family now. Marco treated him much like a brother, and Anabella delighted in seeing him at the table, as she seldom talked with him under other circumstances. Lately, making decorative objects had become a consuming pastime, and she had been creating a large wreath for their front doors. She asked her mother if she could walk to the outbuildings after lunch with Albret to search for vines and other natural objects to complete her wreath.

"I could bring her right back on my horse," suggested Albret, not wanting this opportunity to slip away.

"It would take less than an hour, Mother." Then she added, "I am fourteen now."

"And a responsible fourteen year old you are, Anabella," said Costanza. "You will see that she is back promptly, Albret?"

❧

After quickly grabbing a basket for her treasures, the two walked out the north door and across the grounds, happily chatting about the weather and other innocuous subjects.

Suddenly Anabella turned to her companion. "I do not know when Marco is ever going back to Venice to contact that nobleman he has picked out for me. He and Bianca left this morning without one word about that to me." She shared nearly everything with Albret whenever she had an opportunity.

"You are eager to be betrothed, I see, Anabella. You told me once you never wanted to be married."

"But I am older now. I can think of nothing more wonderful than caring for a husband and tiny babies. If I want to be married by the time I am sixteen, Marco needs to make a choice soon."

"Pardon me if I should not ask, Anabella, but do you think you will love this nobleman he has in mind?"

"I guess there is no way to know until after the betrothal. Marco and Mother will arrange situations where we can meet. And when we are finally betrothed, we will have a gala affair in the ballroom." She walked briskly ahead, swinging her basket.

Albret caught up with her and reached for her hand. She stopped and faced him. "Anabella, forgive me if I speak too boldly, but do you ever think about me?"

A tingling flood of emotion swept over her as she looked directly into his handsome, clean-shaven face. "Yes, Albret, I think about you often." She dropped her long lashes. "But you are not a nobleman. Marco would never consent. . . ."

"I see," said Albret and let go of her hand. "I hope whoever marries you will love you with all his heart."

Anabella did not know how to respond to this. They walked along in silence until she found some pinecones. "These should work fine," she said to the pine tree.

With her basket full, she stood outside the stables while Albret went inside to saddle his horse. She leaned against the building and picked over the objects she had found. Suddenly she became aware of hushed voices. They seemed to be coming from a storage shed next to the stables. Out of curiosity she approached and listened. An open window allowed her to hear distinctly.

"You will be well paid. Every man will have a weapon, either a sword or a pistol."

"But I am a loyal worker. If the castle goes down, I have no job. My family will not eat."

"Listen, you coward. You cannot afford not to join. Everyone else has signed up. You go asking about, and they will take you out, plain and simple."

Terror struck Anabella. Who were these men, and what were they discussing? It certainly sounded ominous.

At the sound of Albret's horse, the voices became silent. Albret helped Anabella to the saddle and jumped on behind. He said nothing, still smarting from their previous conversation.

Anabella spoke only when they were out of earshot of the shed. "Albret, two men were plotting something in that shed. Rather, one was trying to talk the other into joining something where everyone would be paid and have a weapon."

"You are a good little spy, Anabella," he said as a sincere compliment. "Do not turn your head completely, but see if you can identify that man riding off toward the river."

"I think that is Anslo!" she said with terror in her voice. "We are in for more trouble. And Marco left this morning."

"He probably was watching and saw your brother leave. Anslo knows how to slip through the woods by the river and not be detected by any of the posted guards. The land is too vast to cover all points."

After Anabella quoted the exact words of the conversation as she remembered it, Albret concluded that "everyone has signed up" was just a bluff. "Your mother and I have made a point of knowing every one of the workers and guards, as well as the household servants. I believe their loyalty will hold."

&

Costanza relived the excursion with Antonio to the cascades many times. Over and over she heard his voice saying, "Costanza, I love you." *I know I love Antonio, but I could not bring myself to tell him. This constant longing for his presence is nearly unbearable. Will he return? When? And if he comes, he will stay only long enough to increase the longing when he leaves.* She remembered the words of Clarice: *I think it is better not to have people in your life who you are always missing.*

Antonio did return. Unexpectedly. The guard announced his presence as Costanza was leaving the study for the noontime meal. She met him in the reception room and invited him to join her, Anabella, and Albret at the little table in the inner courtyard. The dead leaves of winter had carefully been raked away. Spring flowers bloomed in Grecian urns and along the paths. The fountain in the center spouted a tall stream upward while shorter spurts circled around it.

"And what is your destination this time, Signore Turati?" asked Albret when they were all seated and served.

"Actually, this is my destination this time," he answered, sounding somewhat embarrassed to come there with no apparent purpose. "I left my merchandise in Rome with Paolo. He is proving himself quite good at sales."

"Then you will return to Rome?" asked Costanza. She remained puzzled as to his purpose in coming. But whatever his reason, her heart sang within her breast, and she longed to feel his strong arms around her.

"More likely, I will meet up with the train on its return to Florence," he said and paused to take a bite of food. "I am planning a rather extensive trip of several weeks, perhaps a couple of months to Venice and into France. If I do not soon establish trade with Lyon for silk, my clients will seek out other merchants. Italian wool is also sought after in France. Thus I need to establish that route as soon as possible."

"I see," said Costanza.

Conversation continued on a variety of subjects. Anabella's tutor arrived, and she excused herself for her lessons. Albret dutifully returned to his tasks.

After a servant cleared the table, the two remained alone in the courtyard. Antonio, recalling his last visit, remarked, "You have heard no more from the Sculli brothers, I presume."

"Not exactly," she answered, weighing whether she should mention the latest information.

"Do not withhold anything, Costanza. I detect concern in your voice."

"All right; I will tell you. Albret and Anabella overheard what sounded like the plotting of an uprising among the workers. Stirred up, evidently, by Anslo, whom we dismissed. But Albret and I have made an effort to acquaint ourselves with each employee. We have treated them fairly, and not a single one has indicated a problem. We believe they will remain loyal to us."

"Hmm," said Antonio. "But if they are intimidated or bribed or even threatened with harm, each will consider what is best for himself and his family. Perhaps I should stay around until we learn what this is all about," said Antonio, as though this were his castle to defend.

"I do not want to think about that just now." She smiled at him. "I would rather enjoy your company for the moment."

Antonio reached across the table and took her hand. "Let us walk around the gardens. Someone has done a wonderful work of art in designing the plantings."

"Lorenzino drew up the plans many years ago. A gardener does the work, but Anabella is gifted in artistic design and has made several suggestions this spring. Did you notice the large wreath on our front doors?"

"She made that? It is marvelously arranged with all the painted pinecones and such." They strolled along the path hand in hand. Then Antonio stopped and took her other hand also. They stood facing each other, he looking down into her large, upturned eyes.

"Costanza," he said, "I came here today for a specific reason."

"Yes?"

"You remember I told you I loved you when we were at the falls."

How could she forget? She felt her hands dampen within his and blood flush her face. The intensity of her love for this man engulfed her entire being. He put his arms around her and held her close to his body. She breathed in the scent of leather and the scent of the man she loved with all her heart. If only she could remain thus forever.

Antonio pulled back and placed his hands on her shoulders. Even the loss of a few inches between them made her feel deprived.

"Costanza," he said simply, "I love you. Do you love me?"

She looked into his handsome face—the twinkling eyes, the graying mustache, the little pointed beard. "Yes, Antonio, I love you."

Again he pulled her close. "Costanza, I want you to be my wife. Will you? Will you marry me?" Several minutes passed as they stood thus in a warm embrace. Then Costanza pulled away and walked slowly down the path. She seated herself on a stone bench under an arbor of vines. Antonio followed and sat beside her.

"Costanza, you do not have to answer immediately. If you need time to think or discuss it with your children—I am sure they will have an opinion on the subject. But, be assured, I care a great deal for them also. I want you always to remain close with them. Anabella still needs your guidance, and they both will always need your love." He tilted her chin up to look into her face and was alarmed to see, not joy, but tears.

"Costanza, my love, have I upset you?"

"Yes. No. I do love you, Antonio. So much so that I cannot bear to be without you. As a merchant you will be gone much of the time. I should be happy for your opportunity to go to France for two months. But I suppose I am selfish. . . ."

"Few husbands, at least among those I associate with, spend their days at home. A man must work, must strive, must get ahead. Do you not understand that?"

"Yes. I understand that is the way it is. Lorenzino traveled very little, though. I saw him every day."

"Costanza, I am not Lorenzino. You have many skills and talents that, I understand, you have only recently developed. Frankly, I thought at first that was unfeminine. It rather irritated me—your keeping books and making business decisions. But as I have grown to know and love you, I greatly admire those traits. I am proud of what you have done with the seigniory—and Marco is also, I think."

"Antonio, I would give all that up if we could be together. It would not be that important to me." She looked pleadingly up at him.

"You do not need to give up anything, Costanza. We can go on living our lives the way we have." He paused and thought a minute. "Of course, you would live at my new villa in Florence. . . ."

"And leave my little lambs? And my fields of wheat?"

"I will put you in charge of planting my wheat."

"No. That is not the problem. I could leave this estate to go with you to your villa. But, Antonio, I would spend so much time alone. Without you. I know you must travel, that you must do what you have to do. But it is not a life for me. The pain of longing for you would be more than I could bear. If you leave my life, gradually that longing will lessen. I do not want my last years to be lived in sadness. No, Antonio, I must refuse your proposal of marriage."

"Then it will be I who must live his remaining years in sadness. As you might imagine, I have met and courted several women in my life. But never has there been one I cherished so completely. I will never find another Costanza."

"I am sorry to give you pain, Antonio, but I know no other way. We will both go our separate ways, and time will heal our hearts."

"Costanza, will you at least allow me to stay until we determine what is going on with the workers? Anslo has already killed one man, your servant Sandro. What he is stirring up could be personal revenge for his dismissal, or it could relate to the Scullis' vendetta. Either way, you and Anabella are vulnerable here. Especially with Marco in Florence." Even though his heart was torn apart by her refusal, he still wanted to protect her.

"Thank you, Antonio. I know how thoughtful and caring you are, but Marco should be back tomorrow. It was to be a short journey of only a few days." She sat straight, her tears dried, and spoke in her businesslike tone. Already she was retreating from him, desperately seeking her own healing.

"As you will, Costanza," he said. He stood and kissed her hand. "Remember that I will love you forever." With that he turned and walked back through the castle, out the front doors, across the flagstones, and through the gate. He was gone.

Costanza waited a few minutes alone, then went inside and up the staircase. Entering her room, her gaze fell on the elegant beaver hat with turkey feather tips, sitting atop her dresser. She flung herself across the bed and wept bitter tears.

twenty

Late in the afternoon, Albret settled into the window seat in the little alcove by the kitchens. He held a book of Latin verses. This time, however, his interest was not in reading but in hoping Anabella would pass this way. Just as he decided his wait was in vain and rose to leave, she arrived as though by appointment. She wore a dark dress with puffed sleeves and a pale underskirt. Braids circled the crown of her head, and long curls bounced to her shoulders.

"Albret," she said, taking the place next to him on the window seat. "Have you noticed how preoccupied Mother is of late? I did not think she showed enough concern when we told her about Anslo stirring up trouble."

Albret thought his heart would burst with the sweet scent of the girl he adored so near him. He leaned as far into the corner as possible to keep from being completely overwhelmed by their closeness.

"Marco and Bianca were to be back yesterday," she said, unaware of the effect her presence had on him. "What are you going to do to protect us if there is an uprising?" She knew as well as everyone that authorities would step in only after a crime was committed. Even then, honorable men were expected to defend their own assets.

"First of all, I have been doing a lot of praying lately. Beyond that, preparedness is most important. Your mother is very much concerned and actively thinking on the matter, even if she appears preoccupied. She told me to gather all the daggers, swords, and rapiers and have them ready to distribute to those who will fight for us. I have even unlocked the cases containing your father's collection of dress swords. All these have been placed in the ballroom, under the benches.

"Unfortunately, there are no firearms on the premises. Your father, according to your mother, depended heavily on the fidelity of his workers and the fact that, as a man of character, he had no enemies. This castle has never been attacked. Everything depends on how loyal the men feel toward your mother. Hardly any of the present workers knew your father. Some may resent a woman visibly present as the authority over them. At your mother's direction, I am trying to contact each worker alone—which is not easy—and remind him that loyalty is an important part of his employment; and an honorable man defends the family for whom he works."

"I am frightened, Albret."

"This is a most serious matter, Anabella. I do not want you to be frightened, but you overheard with your own ears the danger facing us. I am doing everything in my power to protect you." He wished with all his heart that he had more power and more means of protection.

He relaxed his position and allowed his arm to brush against her sleeve. She did not move away but smiled up at him. "I feel secure with you, Albret, even as we talk about danger."

With that encouragement, he took her hand boldly in both of his. "Anabella, I care very much for you. I pray never to betray your trust."

She closed her eyes, revealing the length of her thick lashes, and turned her full lips toward his. Albret took her into his arms and tasted the pleasure she offered him. The kiss lingered—warm, moist, young, and virgin.

≈

Antonio sat alone at a table at the Bardi Inn, consuming a breakfast of stale bread, cheese, and jam. Grounds floated in the too-strong coffee. He hardly noticed, however, in his depression. Costanza's rejection had left him stunned and heartbroken. In the many ways he had envisioned her answer to his proposal, "no" was not among them.

After leaving her castle, he had ridden all afternoon and arrived here at his rendezvous point just after darkness fell. Having planned to spend more time with the lady he loved, he found himself a full day ahead of schedule. The merchandising train would not arrive from Rome until early this afternoon. He had spent a wretched night of tossing about with little sleep. He finished the terrible coffee and ran his fingers through his hair. Maybe he should go back to his room and try to sleep a bit.

At that moment, a group of men entered the eating area and sat at a table next to his. They talked in low voices, but he could hear the names Ugo and Piero mingled in the conversation. He ordered another tankard of coffee and turned his back to the group. Besides him, no other customers were in the room. Antonio listened.

"We hid the cannon and wagon in the brush behind the hill. Our army will arrive there in small groups—to dispel suspicion—just after sundown."

"Good work, my men. How many can we count on?"

"I would say about forty, if they all make it. They won't get one *scudo* unless they show up and participate."

"And how many turncoats can we count on, Ugo?"

"Anslo says they have all turned to our side. As well they should with what they're being paid."

"And the threat of a slit throat, if they decline." With that remark, Antonio heard muffled guffaws.

"Now listen, men. There must be no blunders. We've already had enough of that."

"I know we take out any of the men in our way, but what about the womenfolk, Piero?"

"Forget the domestics unless they're armed. Women are harmless. Don't waste your time. Now the marchesa and the girl—take 'em hostage. We'll decide their fate later."

"Anabella's mine. Don't a one of you touch her."

"Hush, Niccolini," the others said.

Antonio sat frozen in horror. The Scullis were going to storm the castle! He could easily beat them there with a warning if he left now, but what could he do against an army of forty, plus those at the castle they had paid off? They would have no way of escape. The cannon would break down the outer doors, and axes would hack off the locks of the inner rooms. Even if he warned them before the onslaught, the circle of turncoats would prevent their leaving.

But act he would! *Surely Marco is back by now,* he thought. *Surely there are pistols in the castle. Perhaps Marco can hold them off by firing from the upper tower until I arrive with an army of my own. All my men, even the clerks, who work on the merchandising train are armed and well trained. There should be around thirty coming in this afternoon. They will need time to eat and rest a bit. Two or three men will need to stay with the mules and merchandise. And horses! They will need fresh horses!*

While the Scullis sat and plotted, Antonio paid his bill. He complained loudly to the innkeeper about a problem with his room and persuaded the reluctant man to follow him up the stairs. Once out of the Scullis' earshot, he asked where he could rent horses. The information, as well as confidentiality, was easily obtained with a few gold coins. *Now if only Paolo can get the train here in time!*

❧

Costanza wearily went about her daily tasks: writing notes in the ledger, supervising the domestic staff, inspecting the wheat fields, checking on the health of the lambs, and observing the shearing of sheep. She had hired a new shearer who was to train others in this laborious skill. This morning he avoided eye contact with her and answered her inquiries curtly. None of the workers entered into friendly chatting as had become the custom. Costanza noted this warning sign with alarm.

When she returned to the castle by way of the north door, Pico and Clarice stood, holding hands, waiting for her in the entrance nook. As she had never noticed any sign of affection between the two married servants, she surmised they had something serious to relate, something that required their solidarity.

Following polite, but loud, greetings, Pico whispered, "Signora, we wish to speak to you in private." Costanza removed a key from a large ring attached to her belt. Pico recognized it as the key to the study. He nodded, and the two hurriedly went up the stairs. Costanza, being well aware that walls have ears, took no chances. She wandered through the kitchens, checking this and that, until enough time passed to confuse any watchful eyes. Indeed, she felt tension among the kitchen staff. Were they friends or foes?

Costanza slipped into the study. Pico had already checked for spies behind the furniture. He locked the door. "You may already know, Signora, that there is a conspiracy brewing among all who work for you." He searched her face for confirmation.

"I know," she said simply.

"My wife and I have been working closely with Albret to determine the level of loyalty among the domestics. At risk of our very lives, we have conferred with each and every household servant—Clarice with the women, I with the men. We believe everyone within the castle walls will remain loyal to you. They are very frightened, however, and may turn if invaders actually penetrate the castle walls."

"That has never been done, even during wars with the Spanish," stated Costanza. "You are both so very brave. I know what a gentle and shy person you are, Clarice. Approaching the women on this matter would be especially difficult for you. I thank you both for your courage and loyalty."

"That is our duty, Signora," they said in unison with a slight bow.

"And what of the outside workers? Do you know anything yet?" She looked back and forth at the two who stood before her. Did they know more than they revealed?

"Of course Albret will report directly to you," said Pico, avoiding a distasteful answer.

Surprisingly, Clarice spoke out, though in a trembling voice. "Signora, please forgive me as a bearer of bad news, but some of the wives of the workers, who are domestics, have indicated that all workers have joined with Anslo in this conspiracy."

Pico put his arm around his weeping wife. "There, there, Clarice. God will protect us all." He turned to Costanza and offered the rest of what they had heard. "Albret will tell you when he comes in, but since Clarice has already told you how the workers stand, I might as well tell you the rest. The workers are already armed, most with daggers hidden under their garments. Don't find yourself alone with any one of them."

"Thank you both for the warnings," she said. "Is there anything else?" Since they offered nothing more, she shook hands with each of them. As this was not a common gesture between mistress and servant, the two showed surprise and gratitude.

&

Antonio was well known in the little wayside community, having lodged his team at the Bardi Inn several times as he passed through on this route between Rome and Florence. He found little difficulty renting sufficient horses from the inhabitants. Various stable hands and loafers offered to accompany him in his private war, at no pay, just for the adventure. He weighed the advantages and disadvantages. It would be preferable, he decided, to direct loyal men, whom he knew well and trusted, to a larger force of unknowns. He left no clue to the locale of his mission.

Well past the noon hour Antonio waited. The horses stomped their feet and snorted, sensing they would soon be on the open road. When the men with the train arrived, they would need to unpack the mules, store the merchandise, and eat. They would need to equip the horses with ammunition, food, and drink. No time remained for rest. He paced back and forth in front of the inn. He rejected the temptation to ride out to meet them—that would only deplete the energy his horse needed for the longer ride to Terni. He waited and paced.

❧

Marco and Bianca had not yet returned from their trip to Florence for the reception of Galileo at the palace of the grand duke. They could certainly be in harm's way also. Especially if they had been followed. Costanza worried about their safety but equally worried about confronting an attack on the ancestral castle without Marco.

Albret arrived at the castle midafternoon accompanied by a worker. As the men had not eaten, Costanza ordered food to be brought to the little table in the courtyard. She asked Anabella to join them. Here they could talk privately.

"You remember Massetti, Signora?" said Albret.

"Yes, of course," she said, recognizing the man with the scarred face whom she had rehired. "Please be seated."

As soon as they had been served, Albret began to talk rapidly in a low voice. "Massetti is the only worker who has come forward to talk about the conspiracy. His life is thus in danger. I propose that he be sheltered here within the castle walls. In turn he is an excellent swordsman. The men in domestic service, though thankfully loyal, tend to lack such skill. Thus he will be an important defender of the interior."

Anabella remained silent throughout this meeting. But she kept her gaze transfixed on Albret.

"Signore Massetti, I am grateful to you for your loyalty," said Costanza.

"It is my pleasure to serve you, Signora. You have saved me and my loved ones from abject poverty. Never can I do enough to repay you."

"What can you tell us about the conspiracy? When do they

plan to strike? What is the plan?" Costanza spoke quietly but frantically.

"I can only tell you what I have been told by those who have declared themselves aligned with Anslo, who have become leaders. They pull us aside and threaten us individually. They tell us everyone else has signed up. We are afraid to talk among ourselves. If I am the only servant who has come to you with this knowledge, my guess is that I am the only loyal one."

"What is the plan, Massetti?" said Albret, anxious to get to the heart of the matter.

"They will strike tonight. We were told that an army of one hundred men will storm the castle during the night. We are not to sleep but lie ready. Even those of us who live in Terni are to remain on the premises tonight."

"You say 'we,' Massetti. Do they think you are one of them?" asked Albret.

"I am ashamed to say so, but, yes; I agreed to join out of fear. But, believe me, I would never harm anyone in this castle. You have been good to me."

He swallowed hard and continued to reveal the plan. "They gave me a dagger. Right here it is." He patted the bulge under his vest. "After dark I am to position myself with others—I know not whom—on the outside of the east wall. A ladder will be by the wall. They told me there are steps on the interior side. I do not know, as this is the first time I have been inside."

"I will give you a tour of the castle, with the signora's permission," said Albret. "You will assist Pico and me in directing the defense. It is not practical for so few to attempt to fight a hundred men plus our own workers in hand-to-hand combat outdoors in the dark. Especially when we do not know friend from foe."

"Then we leave the exterior vulnerable to fire and theft," said Costanza, alarm increasing in her voice.

"Yes, but I believe we can prevent loss of life to those who are with us inside. The stone walls are thick and the windows narrow. Even a torch thrown through a window or over the wall can be extinguished if we are prepared. Except for interior rooms, little is flammable. We will have containers of water placed in strategic areas. We must not use the well, as they will see us preparing, but it is easy enough to divert water from the pipe leading to the fountain. Massetti, on the tour I will mark the strategic areas. Pico is organizing the domestics into teams. You help him get the containers of water in place. . . ."

"And sacks to beat out the flames," said Anabella, breaking her silence.

"Yes, Anabella, thank you." Albret smiled at her. Her face reddened, and she lowered her eyelashes.

"And, Massetti, you are in charge of distributing the arms from the cache in the ballroom. Determine the skill of each man, and assign his post accordingly. Let us go," Albret said in a tone that showed mastery of the situation.

As the men rose to go, Albret turned back to the women. "The two of you, as well as Clarice, I assign to the chapel. You will be our warriors in prayer."

"But. . ." Costanza began. She suspected that he assigned them to the most secure room in the castle to keep them out of the way.

"That, Signora, is where you are most needed," said Albret impatiently. "Praying is not the least you can do, but the most. I defer to your wishes, though."

"You are right, Albret," said Costanza. "Let us go to our station, Anabella."

twenty-one

Throughout the late afternoon and into the night, horsemen rode silently in small groups of four and five. At a notched tree along the road to the Biliverti castle, they veered left and disappeared into the brush. There they gathered around a wagon that held a small cannon, and the Sculli brothers, headed by Piero, plotted and planned the storming of the castle.

&

Finally, Antonio's merchandising train arrived, much later than he had hoped. But his men hurriedly carried out the preparations, imbued with the excitement of battle. So as not to appear as an army, they split into groups of about ten, each with a leader and a scout who would circulate among the divided groups.

&

At the castle, preparations continued at a brisk rate. Signals to alert the others, with a variety of messages, were learned by all. Materials to quench fire sat ready. Albret retrieved the ladder placed at the east wall and poured oil on the inner stairs. In case the enemy scaled the wall, they would find a slippery descent on the other side. A man or woman stood posted at nearly every window. Costanza, Anabella, and Clarice took turns leaving the altar to continue praying, eyes open, at the chapel window.

As it grew dark, candles were lit only in the inner hallways and staircases—no light at the windows. When all was ready, Albret slipped into the chapel. "Everything and everyone is in place. There is no more we can do," he told the women in a confident tone. "It is now in the hands of God."

"I do not understand why this is happening," said Costanza,

"but I know God will be with all of us in whatever we face." Clarice continued to pray at the altar.

"We will pray without ceasing," said Anabella. Albret took her hand in the darkness. "I will carry you in my heart throughout this night," he whispered.

"And you will be in mine," she answered. He squeezed her hand and was gone. Costanza heard the exchange, secretly happy to know they cared for each other.

Anticipation intensified as the night hours dragged on. Pico grew weary at his station by the front staircase window. Suddenly he saw movement coming up the road. He pounded a brick twice against the floor to signal an approach at the front. Albret ran up the stairs.

"What do you see?"

"In the distance there." Pico pointed. "It appears to be a very large carriage, moving slowly. It must be Marco."

"I hope you are right. But it looks too large for a carriage." At a certain point, the vehicle moved as a silhouette against the dim sky. "Pico, look!" Albret said, terror choking his voice. "That is the outline of a cannon!"

"We are doomed," moaned Pico.

They watched as if in a trance as horses pulled the wagon to a position facing the front doors. Five or six men appeared to be setting it in place.

"The signal for 'take cover'—what is it?" asked Pico.

"Three quick thumps, a pause, and a very loud one." Albret picked up the brick and pounded it as he spoke. This was one of the least practiced signals since no one had expected a cannon to break down the doors!

❧

Antonio's three groups of warriors converged after passing through Terni. Antonio rode in the lead, bearing a standard at the end of a pole for all to follow. They stopped briefly for final instructions. "I have no idea what we will encounter, men, when we arrive. I fear we may be too late. If I signal to surround the castle, this group go to the left, this one to the right. My group will cover the front gate.

"Remember—take a life only when yours or another's is threatened. Life is more precious than property. Many of the men you will encounter have been intimidated into service. They may hold no ill against anyone but fight only from fright. Those of us who bear firearms, fire often skyward to scatter the enemy. Now before we go into battle, let us pray: Heavenly Father, thank You for caring about us, weak humans that we are. We believe You go into battle before us because ours is a just cause. We pray that your Holy Spirit will hover over the Biliverti castle and protect all those within. I pray for protection for all of these men who so valiantly go forth to protect the innocent from evil. In the name of Your Son, Jesus Christ. Amen."

"Amen," said his men.

⊱

The signal to take cover was repeated around the interior of the castle until, finally, the bellman heard it and pulled the bell rope which was to be the signal of invasion. Costanza rushed to the door to lift the bar for others to take refuge in the chapel. Suddenly a huge *boom* shook the walls. The women covered their ears and knelt with their heads to the floor. After several minutes, a second *boom!* Then a crashing noise below! The sound of heavy boots echoed throughout the castle.

Hefty steps of several men pounded down the corridor toward the chapel. Costanza quickly dropped the latch, locking the door again. It was no use. They were trapped. An ax battered against the lock. The wood splintered, and the lock hung open. A hand reached through and lifted the latch. In the darkness, they heard metal scrape against metal and the door creak open. A man holding a lantern kicked Clarice aside. "You're nothing," he scoffed.

"But here's the prize!" shouted another man triumphantly

as he pulled Costanza from the floor where she knelt. He twisted her hands behind her and tied her wrists.

Still a third man grabbed Anabella and held his hand over her mouth. He dragged her to him with his arm across her chest. "This little wench is mine, all mine." He gloated as he pulled her down the hall.

That is Niccolini's wicked voice, thought Costanza, more worried about her daughter than herself. *We are overrun with enemies. Where is God? Where are our loyal friends?*

A shot from a pistol rang out. More shots followed. "Receive my spirit into Your rest, Lord Jesus," prayed Costanza aloud. Another shot rang out, this time within the chapel. The man holding her lost his grip and let her fall.

"You despicable coward!" she heard a voice say. "Get out of here and join your cronies who fled before you!" The men rushed out of the chapel, bumping into each other in their eagerness to get past the door.

"Antonio, Antonio! Can that be you?" she cried out.

"Indeed it could be," Antonio said, slashing with his rapier the rope that bound her hands. "It is almost over, Costanza. Be strong." They heard the clashing of swords and angry words, coming from down the hall.

"Antonio, Niccolini has carried off Anabella. I fear for her," sobbed Costanza. "Please rescue her."

"I did that once before, Costanza." He held her close. "That is Albret in combat with Niccolini. Let it be his honor to rescue her this time."

The clashing of steel and the angry voices suddenly stopped. Anabella rushed into the room. "Mother, are you all right?" She threw her arms around her mother and Antonio in a three-way embrace.

"Yes, Anabella; Antonio has saved my life. Are you hurt?"

"No, just terribly frightened. Come see how Albret has conquered Niccolini."

Antonio picked up the discarded lantern, and the three of

them stepped out into the hall.

"What shall I do with this insolent coward, Anabella?" Albret asked, as he stood over his foe with one foot placed on his chest. His sword pinned one sleeve to the wooden floor. Antonio held the light over the defeated Sculli. His face lay distorted in fright.

"I say tie him up. We can deliver him to the authorities with a list of the crimes he has committed," she said firmly. "Let justice prevail!"

&

At the first pale light of dawn, they could see the extensive damage to the castle. The ancient front doors had been completely demolished by the two cannonballs. Fragments of Anabella's decorative wreath lay scattered about. Several locks had been hacked open. Debris of every sort was spread across the floors. Spilled water pooled in various places, testimony to invaders scrambling in the dark, tripping over vats, to flee the gunfire.

A little at a time, the night's events were pieced together as everyone told his part of the story. The most encouraging news of all concerned the workers. The sound of the first cannonball was the intended signal for them to storm the castle along with the Sculli army which, incidentally, proved to be far smaller than forecast. At the signal the workers all shouted, "Long live the Bilivertis!" and refused to enter. While waiting in the dark, one by one they had admitted they did not want to rise up against Signora Costanza, who had always treated them fairly.

Very little fighting actually took place. Antonio and his men arrived just after the cannonballs shot through the door. Only the Scullis and a half dozen others entered. Their forty or so hired fighters had hidden in the tall grasses or behind trees not far from the castle. They were scheduled to storm in along with the workers, but at the sound of gunfire they froze.

Pico and Massetti captured Piero Sculli as he fled from the castle. It was he who had bound Costanza. They also captured

Anslo with ease as he frantically tried to make the workers follow his instructions. When Albret marched Niccolini downstairs, they put the three captives in a carriage and proceeded to escort them to authorities at the prison in Terni. Unfortunately, the other two Sculli brothers fled with their army. With the courts now involved, however, apprehending the other two should prove a simple matter.

Six men in isolated combat received wounds worthy of treatment. With help from two of her female servants, Costanza quickly set up her infirmary where she cleaned and bound up their cuts. None needed to stay for further care.

No one had slept that night, and now they were all too energized by the excitement and telling of stories to think of sleep. Antonio told all the domestics and the men he had brought, as well as a few of the workers who stayed around, to sit down at the servants' tables. He and Paolo then served them boiled rice, jam, cheese, and caffelatte which they had prepared themselves in the kitchens. Costanza, after freshening up a bit, made a speech to the rescuers. She praised them for their bravery, loyalty, and goodness. She told her staff to take the whole day off—except for some of the castle guards who would take their turn an-other day. The workers would have the same except for a small crew to care for the animals. They too would have their day later. There would be bonuses for all. They enthusiastically applauded and chanted, "Long live the Bilivertis!"

Afterward, Costanza insisted that Antonio and Paolo sit down, and she and Anabella served them, their liberators. She asked Clarice to sit at the family dining table also. She hoped the gesture would make up for the insult of the invader who had told Clarice she was "nothing." Albret, Pico, and Massetti returned from delivering their captives in time to join them.

No sooner had they been served than Marco and Bianca burst through the shattered doors, shock written across their pale faces. Marco was torn with remorse as he surveyed the devastation. "Three times, Mother, I have left you vulnerable.

Each time tragedy has struck you and Anabella. Can you forgive me one more time?"

"Marco, there is no cause to feel guilt," said Costanza, embracing them both. "Remember, I sent you off with my blessings. God has protected us through all this tribulation. No life has been lost. I know you will want to hear everything, and everyone is eager, I believe, to retell his part in all this."

Indeed they were, talking at the same time as the other, adding details that had been left out, exaggerating a bit here and there. As the narrative culminated with Costanza's telling how Antonio prepared and served breakfast for all, Bianca said, "That is a ghastly but triumphant event you have all lived through. I could not believe it if I did not see this devastation all around me. It may be hard to think of anything else, but Marco has some good news to share with you." All eyes turned toward him.

"Yes, I do. We have two reasons for being so late in our arrival. Of course, had I known of this lurking danger, I would have bypassed the first reason. The reception for my professor, Galileo, at the palace of the duke proved fantastic in all regards. It lasted three days, as you know, with feasting and speeches, as well as other marvelous activities. We met many people who are doing wonderful things."

"My friend from Rome, Artemisia, was there," interjected Bianca. "The duke is quite taken with her painting. I think he may purchase one."

Marco continued with his news. "Among the people we met was a merchant-banker from Madrid, Spain. You will not believe this! When he heard my name was Biliverti, he asked if I could be related in any way to the late Jacopo Biliverti."

The group gasped. It was he whose debt to the Scullis had provoked all the recent catastrophes.

"The banker said Jacopo had purchased a fine palace in Madrid, but at his death no surviving relatives could be found. He listed no one as an heir. The bank has recently sold the property. He had many outstanding debts at the time of his death, including money owed the bank. After the legitimate creditors have been paid, the remainder will go to our estate, if I can show proof of my identity—which, of course, I can. I stayed over an extra day just to consult with this banker."

"That certainly solves one mystery," said Costanza. "I could never figure out how anyone could spend a fortune—enough to last a lifetime—in just a few years. So Jacopo bought a palace for his lavish lifestyle."

"The banker will send a message to me when the account has been settled. At first, I thought all of us could travel to Spain, but—well, we have some other wonderful news. Bianca will tell you about that."

"Yes," Bianca said, blushing. "I will not be traveling anywhere for awhile. Because, Mother Costanza, you are going to be a grandmother. And, Anabella, you will be an aunt."

Spontaneous joy burst forth from all, especially Anabella and Costanza who threw their arms around her. Questions tumbled out from both of them, and graciously Bianca answered them.

"That is another reason for our lateness. I became ill riding so long. We needed to travel fewer hours a day. But I am feeling quite well this morning and very happy to be home—even among all this rubble."

"Will you let me care for the baby? Please, Bianca, I will be ever so careful," said Anabella.

"Of course. I know you will be a tender, loving aunt. You will spoil my baby, if Mother Costanza does not do it first." They all laughed joyfully.

"We will set about immediately making a nursery," said Costanza, beaming with pride.

"This means, Mother, that Bianca and I wish to stay at home for the next few years. We cannot be traveling about with a baby." It was evident that Marco sincerely wanted to do the best for his family.

"I could not be more pleased," said the grandmother-to-be.

twenty-two

Fatigue finally set in on the little group. Marco and Albret hung a huge canvas over the gaping hole that used to be the entrance doors. Unlike the others, Marco and Bianca had spent a restful night at an inn in Terni. Thus, while the others rested, Marco made a thorough assessment of the damage and gathered up any valuables that lay scattered about. Complete cleaning and repairs would begin the next day.

Costanza lay across her bed, but her mind swirled with so many thoughts that she could not sleep. Finally, she resolved the most persistent conflict—Antonio. She could never get this fascinating man out of her mind. If his proposal still held, she would agree to marry him and endure the longing for him during his travels—in exchange for the sublime moments of togetherness. With her mind made up, she fell into a restful sleep.

At midafternoon she got up and refreshed herself. She chose to wear a rose-colored dress with pearl buttons trimming the bodice. Wide pleats draped from the pointed waist over a pale pink underskirt. The hanging oversleeves and upstanding collar with open throat flattered her full figure. As usual, she arranged her hair in a bun high on the crown, with hanging tendrils framing her face. No doubt sometime today she would cross paths with Antonio Turati.

As she descended the stairs, she heard distant strains of music. Following them—for, indeed, she knew who would be playing the lute—she found the source in the courtyard.

Antonio had also dressed with thoughts of seeing the lady he loved. Why else would he have strapped his lute and a small traveling bag behind his saddle to ride off into battle?

His attire was entirely black except for his white, lace-trimmed wing collar, and knee-length leather boots. A short cape draped his right shoulder. He looked up as she approached but continued to sing an Italian love song—*amore mio!* She sat on the bench beside him.

After a few minutes, he set down his lute and looked into her sparkling eyes. "Who could guess you are a lady who survived a stormed castle, capture, and bound wrists only a few short hours ago?" said Antonio, taking her hand in his. "You are a most charming and beautiful lady. Never have I seen you so radiant. I must ask Bianca to paint your portrait as you are at this moment."

"Then she must include you in the picture, for without your bravery, Antonio, I would not even be sitting here at this moment," she said. "I owe my life to you."

"Costanza, we owe everything to the Lord God of heaven. Albret told me how you, Anabella, and Clarice prayed through the night. I prayed with my men on our last stop before arriving here in time. I no longer have any doubt in my mind that God cares for us, weak humans that we are. His Spirit surrounded us throughout the conflict. Did you not feel it?"

"Yes," said Costanza. "But, I will admit to you, for a few moments I doubted, before I heard your voice."

"I shudder to think if I had been only a few minutes later," he said, cherishing the sight of his beloved unharmed before him. Then turning to another subject, he said, "Marco and Bianca brought such wonderful news. Your recovered fortune and then the baby."

"It is very good news, is it not?" she said, looking into his eyes. "Antonio, do you want to marry a grandmother? I have been thinking, and I. . ."

"I have been thinking too, Costanza. You remember I told you I would love you forever. Well, forever is not long enough when you consider our age. And if I travel, if we are apart, then there is even less time in our forever."

That is what I tried to tell you, she thought but said nothing.

"Costanza, I have decided to allow Paolo to buy out my merchandising business over time. He is quite astute. I would feel very comfortable with his taking over. Being so poor as a child, I needed to prove myself, to rise to the top in the business I knew best. I have done that. Now I can be content to gaze on my lovely wife every day of the year—forever. Will you marry me, Costanza?"

"Yes, Antonio, nothing could bring me more joy than to be with you. And I will be delighted to live at your villa in Florence or Rome or wherever you wish, as long as I am with you."

"We could keep the place in Rome, but I would like to make a home in Florence. We can furnish it together. Anabella can come live with us, of course. With her talents in decoration, she will make important contributions. I think she will love the activity in the city."

"She has such an adventurous spirit," said Costanza, pleased that he assumed Anabella would be with them. "She loved everything about Rome, even selling our needlework in the marketplace. The large buildings and huge fountains, the piazzas and statues, fascinated her. But the poor beggars on the street broke her heart."

"Costanza, I have an idea, if you agree. I would love to take in poor children from the street—a few at a time. Nourish them to good health and eventually find apprenticeships for them—as that kind couple did for me years ago. As I told you before, I have tried my hand at this occasionally, but being away so much of the time made it difficult for the child."

"That would be wonderful, Antonio. You know how nursing people to good health has always appealed to me. I could teach them too, or you could bring in a tutor. Certainly I could offer them some mothering," she said with enthusiasm.

"It all sounds so perfect," she continued. "Now that Marco and Bianca are starting a family, they want to stay home at the castle. Frankly, that worried me at first. I have managed so well without Marco that we might run into more clashes in decision making if we both lived under the same roof. They will do much better with me out of their way in Florence."

"Have you consulted your children about our marriage?"

"No, Antonio; I only made the decision upstairs a little while ago," she said with a laugh. "I do not really need their permission, but I do hope for their blessing. I believe Anabella has accepted you. I know she is grateful for all you did last night."

"Shall we then make an announcement at dinner tonight?"

"With pleasure."

Antonio took her in his arms, drew her close to him, and kissed her long and fervently.

❧

Meanwhile, Marco sat with Albret in the study, poring over the list of repairs that needed to be made. They would need to seek out skilled wood-carvers for the front doors and carpenters and locksmiths for the interior doors.

"While all this work is going on, we might as well refurbish the ballroom. Mother and Anabella want to open it for social events—perhaps an impending betrothal," said Marco, laying aside the repair list and turning to Albret.

Albret immediately thought of the childless widower in Venice. Had Marco already concluded this alliance? His heart sank. He had always known that his love for Anabella could never be fulfilled. But knowing could not cushion the blow.

"Albret, Mother tells me she has noticed your affection toward Anabella," began Marco.

"I have never done anything dishonorable!" gasped the young man.

"No, no, that is not what I mean," said Marco. "Mother and I would like to suggest the betrothal of Anabella to you, Albret."

"How can this be? I am flattered beyond reason," said Albret, finding it difficult to adapt to this sudden reversal of his emotions. "I am not of noble birth—you know that. Did you say you want Anabella betrothed to me?"

"Exactly that, Albret. I know of no more honorable and considerate candidate. You did rescue her from a dire fate. You are gifted in so many areas: overseeing the workers, instilling sincere loyalty in them, quickly learning any skill, keeping the ledgers—when Mother allows it.

"You are of noble character, which is far more important than noble birth. My own dear Bianca is from a landed family, and her father is a banker. But they are not of noble blood. Yet she exceeds the qualities of all the noblewomen I have met.

"We feel you will contribute much to the prosperity of this seigniory. We want Anabella to be happy, and we believe she will be very happy with you as her eventual husband. In addition to the dowry, we will offer you and Anabella a portion of the seigniory at the time of marriage. You must realize, of course, that the marriage will not be consummated for two years. Many girls marry at her age, and she is a mature young lady, but we think fourteen is too young. For that matter, you are young to take on such a great responsibility."

Albret wiped the perspiration from his youthful brow. "I agree. Please be assured, Marco, that I have loved no other than Anabella. I will always conduct myself honorably toward her." He could hardly contain his joy, so overwhelmed was he at the fulfillment of his dream. "Marco, have you discussed this idea with Anabella?"

"Not as yet. I feel certain she will be pleased, however," said Marco, surprised at this thought. "She would not expect to be part of the decision. But you may tell her yourself, if you wish. Then we will announce your betrothal at dinner tonight."

"I will seek her out now," said Albret, overjoyed with the prospect.

❧

Albret found her preparing dinner with Costanza in the

kitchen. Both enjoyed cooking and serving, although they did so only on Sunday or days off for the kitchen staff. Costanza was preparing a chicken for roasting. Anabella had finished cutting pasta and was heading toward the garden for greens to be used in a fresh salad.

"May I accompany you, Anabella?" he said as she stepped into the hallway.

"Of course, Albret. You are my rescuer, my hero!" she said, delighted to see him. "What an unearthly ordeal that was last night! I want to hear more details about how you delivered those wicked Scullis to the law officials."

"And I am eager to tell you." They strolled out to the garden behind the castle. Together they began plucking the tender leaves of various greens. "Before I get into that, however, I have something to tell you." He took the greens from her hands and placed them in her basket. Then he held her hands in his. "Anabella, I love you with all my heart."

Suddenly, one of the workers who had remained on duty came galloping up on a horse.

"Albret, you must come quickly!" he exclaimed, coming to a halt. "A ewe is having difficulty with lambing. None of us on duty knows how to handle this. We may lose her if something isn't done immediately. You may join me on my horse."

"I must tend to this, Anabella," he said as he looked into those lovely eyes, framed with long lashes. "Remember I love you." He kissed her gently on the lips. The worker turned his head, shocked that the overseer would dare to kiss the Biliverti signorina.

Albret mounted the horse behind the worker, and they galloped off as Anabella stood watching them.

&

Still trembling with the taste of love upon her lips, Anabella set the plates and silver on the table. She glanced often toward the north door, hoping for Albret to walk in any minute. Antonio assisted Costanza in pulling the chicken from the oven. He remained in the kitchen mostly to be with her. They chatted and laughed at remarks that would not be thought funny by anyone else. Marco entered the dining hall and did his part by lighting the many candles of the candelabra.

" 'Bella, you seem to be in a bright mood. Has Albret spoken to you?" he said, eager to know her reaction to the proposal.

"Yes, he most certainly has," she said with a blush on her cheeks. "You know, Marco, he is a very brave and honest man." She looked to be sure Marco was listening closely. Whether their love could blossom or not depended entirely on her brother's wishes. "He loves me."

"Is that a fact?" said Marco.

twenty-three

Costanza held dinner for as long as was feasible for Albret's return. Anabella was surprised when Albret's mother, Sylvia, accompanied Bianca to the table. So many strange mixings of servant and master had occurred recently, however, that she thought only a little of it and chatted pleasantly with her. When Bianca, who had been resting, came to the table, Marco said, "It is nearly dark. I suggest we begin. Albret will surely be here shortly. Let us pray."

When they lifted their heads from prayer, Albret walked in. He greeted his mother and took the place across from Anabella and announced to all that ewe and twin lambs were doing fine. They praised Albret for his fine work.

He smiled at Anabella throughout the meal as though he wanted to say something to her beyond, "More pasta, please."

When all were finished, Bianca cleared the plates.

"Compliments to our esteemed chefs," said Antonio, lifting his goblet.

"To the esteemed chefs," chimed in the others.

"And now a toast to the betrothal of Anabella and—"

Anabella's mouth fell open in stunned disbelief. "No, Marco, no! I refuse this betrothal! I love Albret with all my heart and will not marry another! I will go to a nunnery first!" She covered her face with her hands and burst into tears.

" 'Bella, sweet sister, you said Albret had spoken. . ."

"Let me speak now," said Albret. Anabella heard the scraping of a chair against the floor and soon felt Albret's presence at her side. He took her hands from her face and pulled her up, facing him.

"Anabella, I thought I would be back in time to finish what

166

I started to say to you in the garden." He then knelt before her, still holding her hands. "Anabella, Marco is talking about your betrothal to *me*. He has asked me to be your husband. Our mothers are in total agreement. Will you agree to marry me? I love you so much."

Anabella smiled sweetly, embarrassed at her recent outburst. "You, Albret, are the one? There is not a man more noble. Yes, I accept this betrothal with joy. I would not do well in a nunnery." She looked back and forth between her mother and Bianca. "You all knew, did you not? No one ever tells me anything," she declared. "But this time I guess it is worth the shock to hear it first from the man I love."

Everyone talked at once. Anabella accepted the many apologies offered her for failing to mention the impending betrothal announcement. "We all thought you should speak first on the matter, since we assumed you knew," said Costanza.

Anabella turned to Sylvia and said with all sincerity, "I am pleased you will be my mother-in-law. Albret's fine qualities are the ones you have instilled in him, I am sure. We can get to know each other better now that Bianca and Marco will be staying home."

"I am very pleased for you and Albret," said Sylvia. "I know you are a young woman who will bring much happiness to his life."

"Sylvia and I will arrange for the *impalmare* ceremony at the church a week from Sunday to make it official between the families," said Costanza, beaming. "After that, we will begin to plan the betrothal ceremony with an extravagant dinner and a ball following."

"In the ballroom!" exclaimed Anabella. "Do you hear that, Albret? We will be the first honored couple to dance at a gala in our refurbished ballroom."

Antonio stood and proposed a toast to the happy couple: "May God's blessings be showered upon you both. May you enjoy health, happiness, and prosperity—and many beautiful children to sit around this table someday."

Everyone cheered and added their own encouraging words. "And now," said Albret, standing, "I thank you all for your good wishes, and especially Marco and Signora Biliverti for welcoming me into their family. But my betrothed-to-be and I would like a few minutes alone, if you will excuse us."

Anabella rose to join him, but Antonio said, "Wait—before you go, your mother and I have an announcement of our own to make. Costanza, I defer to you."

Albret and Anabella returned to their seats. "Well," said Costanza as she folded her hands and looked into the faces of her children, "there is to be another wedding in this family. The barone and I. We ask for your blessing."

"This is startling news!" said Marco. "I had no idea—I—but, of course, Mother, you have my wholehearted blessing. Bianca and I have prayed that you would marry again. But when I mentioned that matter to you once, you remember, you reacted as though it were a topic to avoid completely."

"I remember," said Costanza with a twinkle in her eye. "But that was before I met Antonio Turati." She then looked to Anabella, concerned about her feelings.

"Mother," said her daughter, "the barone saved my life. Then he saved yours. I believe he is someone we should keep around always. I know much more about love now than I did before. You both have my blessing also."

Antonio went to the kitchens and brewed his caffelatte for all. "The only way to end a fine dinner among loved ones," he said. Costanza shared their plans for taking in poor, abandoned children at Antonio's villa. Anabella could at once see her role in helping. She was also pleased that Antonio had enough confidence in her to help with decorating ideas. She thought moving to Florence an exciting idea, but it pained her to be separated from Albret for two long years.

"I will write to you often," said Albret, equally concerned

by the thought of not seeing her every day. "And, when Marco permits, I will come for a visit."

"You and Mother Costanza will return when our baby is born," said Bianca to cheer her. "Perhaps you can stay even a few months longer after your mother leaves."

"I am not yet ready to give you up completely," said Costanza. "I have not finished my mothering."

"Does a mother ever?" said Marco with a knowing laugh.

"I will soon know about that," said Bianca. "I am so pleased with all the wonderful news, but I must bid all of you good night. It has been a very long and tiring day."

The little group dispersed. Albret and Anabella found their alcove and sat talking of their future far into the night.

❧

Antonio and Costanza walked in the moonlight in the court-yard. "Our lives have changed so drastically and so quickly," said Costanza. "Less than a year ago, I awoke to flames destroying the vineyards. Add to that the loss of cattle, the loss of fortune, and the near loss of my child. We have been menaced by evil and attacked by our enemies. Yet the Lord has been good. He has given me so much. I never thought I could love again. And here you are, giving up your business and refusing to let me go."

"You have become stronger and even more lovable through your tragedies," said Antonio as he took her hand. "God has been good to me also. You, dear Costanza, have taught me how to trust in Him. We will be a great team as we work with the street urchins. We have a lot of planning to do. Paolo and my men will set out in the morning to meet up with my merchandising train and head back to Florence."

"You will stay a few days, at least, will you not? We have not even set a wedding date."

"Tonight would not be soon enough," he said, tilting her face toward his. "You are so beautiful in the moonlight. Yes, I will stay a few days. We must make decisions, arrange things, make lists, and all of that. But, Costanza, our forever has already begun."

He put his hands on her shoulders and gently slid them down her back to her waist. He pulled her close to his body and kissed her long and tenderly.

"Antonio, my love, forever with you can never be long enough," she whispered.

A Letter To Our Readers

Dear Reader:

In order that we might better contribute to your reading enjoyment, we would appreciate your taking a few minutes to respond to the following questions. We welcome your comments and read each form and letter we receive. When completed, please return to the following:

Rebecca Germany, Fiction Editor
Heartsong Presents
PO Box 719
Uhrichsville, Ohio 44683

1. Did you enjoy reading *The Heart Knows* by Elaine Bonner?
   ❑ Very much! I would like to see more books
     by this author!
   ❑ Moderately. I would have enjoyed it more if
   _____

   _____

   _____

2. Are you a member of **Heartsong Presents**? Yes ❑ No ❑
   If no, where did you purchase this book?_____

   _____

3. How would you rate, on a scale from 1 (poor) to 5 (superior), the cover design?_____

4. On a scale from 1 (poor) to 10 (superior), please rate the following elements.

   _____ Heroine   _____ Plot

   _____ Hero   _____ Inspirational theme

   _____ Setting   _____ Secondary characters

5. These characters were special because_____

_____

_____

6. How has this book inspired your life?_____

_____

_____

7. What settings would you like to see covered in future
   Heartsong Presents books?_____

_____

_____

8. What are some inspirational themes you would like to see
   treated in future books?_____

_____

_____

9. Would you be interested in reading other **Heartsong
   Presents** titles?   Yes ❑   No ❑

10. Please check your age range:
    ❑ Under 18   ❑ 18-24   ❑ 25-34
    ❑ 35-45   ❑ 46-55   ❑ Over 55

Name _____

Occupation _____

Address _____

City _____ State _____ Zip _____

Email _____

United We Stand

In the global convulsion of World War II, millions of people find their lives in upheaval. From the homeland to the frontlines, American citizens are suddenly diverted off their chosen paths. They'll each fight a war—in their own way and with varying success, but always bound by the same cause. Can they see God's hand—and perhaps find romance—amidst the chaos?

Faith unites these women. . .love gives them strength. Follow their stories through one of the most compelling periods of American history.

paperback, 480 pages, 5 ³/₁₆" x 8"

Repackaging of titles first released in **Heartsong Presents.**

♥ ♥ ♥ ♥ ♥ ♥ ♥ ♥ ♥ ❤ ♥ ♥ ♥ ♥ ♥ ♥ ♥ ♥

♥ ♥ ♥ ♥ ♥ ♥ ♥ ♥ ♥ ❤ ♥ ♥ ♥ ♥ ♥ ♥ ♥ ♥

·······Presents·······

Great Inspirational Romance at a Great Price!

Heartsong Presents books are inspirational romances in contemporary and historical settings, designed to give you an enjoyable, spirit-lifting reading experience. You can choose wonderfully written titles from some of today's best authors like Peggy Darty, Sally Laity, Tracie Peterson, Colleen L. Reece, Lauraine Snelling, and many others.

When ordering quantities less than twelve, above titles are $2.95 each.
Not all titles may be available at time of order.

SEND TO: Heartsong Presents Reader's Service
            P.O. Box 721, Uhrichsville, Ohio 44683

Please send me the items checked above. I am enclosing $_____.
(please add $2.00 to cover postage per order. OH add 6.25% tax. NJ add 6%). Send check or money order, no cash or C.O.D.s, please.
      To place a credit card order, call 1-800-847-8270.

NAME _____

ADDRESS _____

CITY/STATE_____ ZIP _____